PAVEMENT

ANDREW DAVIE

PAVEMENT

All Due Respect
An imprint of Down & Out Books
3959 Van Dyke Rd, Ste. 265
Lutz, FL 33558
www.DownAndOutBooks.com

The characters and events in this book are fictitious. Any similarity to real persons, living or dead, is coincidental and not intended by the author.

Cover design by Eric Beetner

ISBN: 1-948235-99-4
ISBN-13: 978-1-948235-99-0

For my mother, father, and brother.

Gropper entered the bar.

He'd cased it the day before, knew the schedules of the workers, the locations of the entrances, and the delivery times. He was a man who left nothing to chance.

It was close to midnight, and the place was as packed as it was going to be. Gropper took a seat at the bar, ordered a Jack and Coke, and laid the newspaper out next to him.

The jukebox spat out Bob Seger while the scattered groups made idle conversation. The place was a beacon for blue-collar workers and degenerates.

He killed his drink and ordered another. He hadn't shaved for a few days and wore nondescript clothes. No one would be paying him any attention now and, if anyone asked later, they would get a watered-down description.

Gropper checked the time. A patrol car would be in the neighborhood for the next half an hour.

Good, it would give him time to go over the game plan. He had scoped the bartender the previous day, but up close he could get a good read. The guy wore a sleeveless black T-shirt that barely covered his frame. He had no muscle definition but was prison big. A shaved head glistened in the overhead light, and a two-tone beard hung down to his chest, streaked with gray. The bartender's nose had been broken a few times, and the scar tissue around his eyes suggested he could take a beating and keep coming. Gropper made a note: *If the bartender gets involved, give him the full business right away.*

In the back was the kitchen, which consisted of a grill manned by two ex-cons. They would stay out of it or run at the first sign of trouble.

Gropper hazarded a guess that at least one of the patrons might join the fray, if it lasted long enough, another reason to keep things contained and expedited. No sermons, no acquiescing to pleas or apologies—just execute the job.

He would act quickly and be in the wind.

His target would be in the back office. A loaded .38 in the top desk drawer, ledger in the second, petty cash box in the third.

Gropper ordered a final drink to bring him to an even keel. The adrenaline wouldn't start coursing until right before the deed, but he felt it building, like a race car driver revving the engine. A group of people paid the bill and left. In total, there were now nine, including Gropper, in the entire place. He clocked them out of the corner of his eye. They were already drunk, busy arguing about which of them had a harder week. If things broke his way, he'd only have to deal with two of them. If not, possibly four or five. He'd dealt with worse.

He began folding the newspaper.

The bartender was engrossed in the news on the TV, but if he had noticed, Gropper would have looked like another drunk trying to escape the monotony. In reality, he was making a weapon. He'd read about how in the sixties, in Millwall, England, the police cracked down on soccer hooligans. Before fans could enter the stadium, they had to give up rolls of mints, pens, combs, boots, and shoelaces. But some enterprising fans brought newspapers with them. When rolled up and folded, they had created what became known as a Millwall brick. Gropper dug into his pocket for two rolls of pennies and laid them toward the top of the paper, so they would give the thing some heft. He finished folding it over.

"Hey," Gropper called out. He gripped the improvised weapon in his right hand.

"Yeah?" the bartender said without taking his

3

eyes from the screen.

"Let me get one more."

The bartender didn't move for a moment, then fixed the drink and set it in front of Gropper. When he turned, Gropper hit him on the side of the head with the brick. The bartender slouched and Gropper hit him a second time in the face, breaking his nose and sending him to the ground.

"Hey, I think something's wrong," Gropper called out to the other patrons. The group at a table in the back stopped talking and looked over.

"I'm going to call nine-one-one."

Gropper was up and off his stool, heading to the back before anyone could say anything.

"Five-o! Five-o!" he yelled through the swinging doors into the kitchen. He didn't think the ex-cons would interfere, but again, you never knew. He was through the hallway and outside of the office. He rapped loudly a few times on the door. Footsteps approached. As it opened, he heard, "Jesus Christ, what the—"

Gropper hit the man in the chest with the Millwall brick. The man fell backward and scrambled for the desk and the .38 he had stored there.

The guy was Joe, the manager. He had a thick mustache, sideburns, and white, powder-caked his nostrils. He crawled quickly and wheezed as his

4

lungs fought to displace carbon dioxide. He wasn't a pro, but he was savvy enough to go for the weapon. He pulled the drawer out, but Gropper was already there, kicking it shut. It crunched Joe's hand. He yelled, then crumpled to the floor. Gropper flipped him onto his back and gripped him by the shirt.

"My hand," Joe said and stared at it. Multiple bones had been broken, and the webbing of his ring and middle fingers was severed. His face was ashen, and he was shaking. Shock would set in soon.

"Listen," Gropper said, "You fenced a ring and bracelet. Where's the locket?"

Joe looked at him, eyes blank, uncomprehending.

Gropper took Joe's injured hand and squeezed. Joe's eyes rolled back into his head, and he was on the verge of passing out.

"Cashbox."

Gropper tore the third drawer open, grabbed the box, and headed for the door. He could cut through the kitchen and out the back. One of the other customers blocked the entrance, a squat man with a scowl and a head the shape of a bullet. He didn't make any threats, just started swinging. Gropper knew instantly this guy had no finesse—too much time on the heavy bag. Probably uttered profane things as he slugged it.

The guy fired a decent combination, most of which Gropper took on his forearms. He landed a counter right hand, then kicked the guy in the shin with his steel-toed boot. The guy winced and slunk down. Gropper hit him with a one-two, and the guy fell to his side, a marionette with its strings cut.

The rest of the crowd stayed in the bar, and Gropper could see them debating what to do. He didn't wait to find out. He moved through the swinging doors, past the grill, and out into the parking lot through the service entrance.

He continued through the bushes, onto the sidewalk, and down a side street. He got to the highway. At this time of night, a few cars drove by, but mostly there was an eerie silence. Gropper continued across the highway into the strip mall. The bail bonds office, pizzeria, nail salon, and Mexican restaurant were all closed. He found his car parked where he'd left it, in front of a dental office.

Once inside, he calmed his breathing, listening for the telltale sound of a siren. Nothing yet. It would probably take them another few minutes, and by then, he would be long gone.

"How'd it go?"

McGill took a massive bite of his corned beef

sandwich and chased it with the rest of his Mickey's. He was on his second course of what would probably be three to four entrées. The diner was McGill's favorite and the only place he'd meet. Rumor was he never left the place. Gropper took a sip of his coffee. He never ate during these meetings.

"Fine," Gropper said.

McGill sneered—his way of smiling. He sat back in his seat, and the leather squealed. McGill was an enormous man whose appetites had ravaged what had been a formidable person. His once-imposing frame now looked overstuffed as he pushed three hundred pounds. He was a former cop turned unlicensed PI. His career as a legitimate law enforcement officer long gone, he turned to the other side. His Rolodex had enough contacts to keep him well informed about the local Charleston microcosm.

McGill was a fixer now, a middleman. He would find two interested parties, and like a sell side broker, match them up. He would get a taste, of course. He had a legion of hitters, junkies, hookers, and dealers who all got greased for info. Regardless, the reality was McGill was a small timer who kicked back enough to those in power.

McGill never sought the limelight. He wasn't flashy, didn't drive a car that screamed out for attention. He was a smart operator.

Gropper didn't say anything more. McGill's sneer faded. He finished his sandwich in three bites.

"I've always liked the way you do things: lead pipe cruelty, mercenary sensibility."

Gropper's lip twitched; it was the closest he came to laughing. Gropper reached into his pocket and left the envelope containing the locket on the cushion next to him.

McGill signaled the waiter, who brought over his next course and a fresh Mickey's. The beer wasn't on the menu, but it was a concession the owner made for McGill. Gropper sat in silence while McGill ate. Gropper finished his coffee.

"Try some pecan pie. It's the best."

"No, thanks."

"All right, I'll let you know when I need you."

Gropper nodded and left. Later, he would check the dead drop where McGill had left his payment. Gropper went out the service entrance and got into the car.

He'd take a different route home. Along the way, Gropper imagined how it would go down later. McGill would return the locket to his client, in this case, the grandson of the locket's true owner.

When Joe wasn't operating the bar, or holding for a dealer, he did some B and E on the side, as part of a crew of three. He'd fenced most of the jewelry, but the pawn shop owner was on McGill's payroll. Word had already circulated about the items, and the guy alerted McGill almost as soon as Joe had left.

"The locket had sentimental value," McGill said when he gave Gropper the information. Gropper wasn't sentimental, nor did he want to be included in the post-activity festivities. He did not want to receive thanks or be the recipient of hugs and pats on the back for a job well done. Perhaps McGill was on to something with his mercenary comment.

Gropper pulled the car into a spot off the side street near his house. He nodded to a group of men sitting on the stoop next door. They uttered terse acknowledgment of his presence and went back to tilting their brown bags.

Across the street, John lounged in his chair on the second-floor balcony. His brown skin hung off him like putty and glistened from sweat. He was a full-blown alcoholic who rarely left the house. A fifth of vodka stayed between his feet, except when he was sucking at the neck. Gropper paid him fifty bucks a week to keep an eye on both Gropper's car and the comings and goings of people to the house. Gropper sublet a room, which had direct access to the sidewalk.

John saw Gropper and wiped at his nose—the signal to let him know everything was clear and that Gropper had no visitors that day. Gropper unlocked his police lock, felt the crossbar slide, and walked into the dimly lit room.

It was sparse. Practically the same as when he first moved in six months ago: a bed against the far wall underneath a window with an armoire next to it. Otherwise, barren. Gropper had a go bag at the bottom foot of the bed, and another one in a bus station locker a few miles away. If it came down to it, he could be gone in under a minute as if he never existed. The thought gave him a sense of security. He owned nothing, had nothing. He locked the door behind him, replacing the police crossbar out of habit.

Ms. Bradley, age seventy-eight, owned the house. She spent most of her time traveling back and forth to the hospital. Her afflictions were too long to list in one sitting, but she was tough. She and Gropper immediately took to each other. He helped around the house, when he could, and she gave him free reign of the place. Her daughter had worked with McGill, so she knew to keep Gropper's business anonymous.

The house was quiet except for a grandfather

clock that ticked away the seconds. Gropper went into the living room, walked over to the bookcase, and selected a Bill Evans record. He fitted the album on the revolver turntable and placed the needle on track two. He sat down and shut his eyes.

The music was the one pleasure he allowed himself.

McGill took a bite of his pecan pie. They put it on the grill to warm it up first. It was how he always ended the day. Carmine sat back in the booth and opened his arms like flower petals blossoming. He had enough product in his hair for it to shine, Carmine was an emissary for Cleon James. Cleon and his crew had made some noise over the last few years, and he was looking to expand his enterprise. This was the second time Carmine had dropped by the diner. The first time, he told McGill about the group's intentions, offered terms, and McGill listened politely. Then he told Carmine what he told people who'd been trying to shake him down since he set up shop.

"Go fuck yourselves."

Carmine laughed and said to think about it. The terms were reasonable, but they weren't going to remain that way forever.

This evening, Carmine returned and his good nature about McGill's earlier response was not there. This time, he went into specifics of things they had done in the recent past to people who didn't see their way.

"So?" Carmine said, as McGill finished eating.

"My message hasn't changed."

Carmine bit his lower lip, and then laughed like a hyena.

"You know, you're not untouchable," he said. "Some shit could happen to you, same as it does anyone else."

"And what do you think will happen if something bad comes down on me?"

"You think I'm scared of Gropper?" Carmine said, then turned to look to see if Gropper might actually be there. "But I don't see—"

McGill hit Carmine in the sternum. Carmine's eyes bulged from their sockets as the air wheezed from his lungs. His mouth opened and shut a few times like a fish out of water.

"First off, just worry about me. Be glad Gropper isn't here, or you'd be dead."

"You can't…" Carmine began.

"I just did."

Carmine took in a deep breath and coughed.

"Relax, it'll pass." McGill took a toothpick from

the dispenser. Carmine's face turned a shade of green, then his breathing returned.

"You're fucking—"

McGill hit him in the same spot. Carmine was amazed at the speed McGill moved at for a man his size. His eyes widened to the size of half-dollars.

McGill signaled the waiter, who came and took his plate and brought a coffee and water.

"Here, drink this." He nudged the water toward Carmine and took a sip of the coffee. Carmine stared at McGill, unable speak.

"Swallow your pride and go. Next time, Lord help you if Gropper is here."

Carmine looked like he was going to say something but instead rubbed at his chest and headed toward the door.

Maurice liked to take care of business himself. He was stubborn that way; his mother instilled it in him when he was young. Solve your own problems. Having three siblings, two who never saw twenty-one, the advice served him well. Problems not dealt with had a way of quickly growing exponentially worse. Like snuffing out a match versus snuffing out a raging inferno. He considered the calm to always be the signal before the storm. When—not if, but when—a problem occurred, he took care of it straight away.

He had been diagnosed with cerebral palsy at a young age, and his mother also made certain he was capable of taking care of himself and never to accept pity.

He hadn't meant to get into the game. Maurice had promised to steer clear of drugs and drinking, which claimed both his two brothers and his father. He finished high school, then worked as the day shift manager of a motel, and took night classes toward a bachelor's in management.

They said it was the stress of all the years of taking care of her family that finally caused the heart attack. Suddenly, Maurice was responsible for taking care of himself and his younger sister. He attended fewer classes and logged more hours at work. Soon, it felt like he was there twenty-four-seven.

Then his cousin Stacy came to him with a proposition.

Maurice hadn't seen her in almost a year.

She showed up at the motel during the day, still high, but coherent. It looked like she hadn't slept in months.

"Jesus," he said when she got close enough. She hadn't bathed in a while, either.

14

"It's good to see you too, cuz."

"Hey, you can't be here right now." He checked the clock. "My shift ends in an hour. There's a KFC across the highway, I'll meet you there."

She smiled, revealing some busted teeth, and stumbled through the front door. She was in worse shape than he initially thought. Still, she was family, and he felt bad about what she'd been through.

When his shift ended, he met her at the KFC and bought her a chicken tenders and side of fries. They caught up for about twenty minutes, and then she laid it on him.

Maurice said no. He didn't want to do anything illegal. The promise to his mother still weighed heavily on him. Stacy sighed.

"I'm not asking you to get your hands dirty."

"I can't do it. Besides, what do I know about prostitution?"

"You know how to manage things, right?" Stacy said. She sat across from him, hair pulled back into a ponytail. She wore just enough makeup to accentuate the beauty she had left. She was in her late twenties but looked like she was in her forties.

"Yes, but there's a difference."

"I know the ins and outs. I can handle the money, recruiting, the day to day."

"So why do you need me?"

She sat forward. Under the direct light, he could see remnants of scars and her heavy use of concealer. "It's medieval out there. I need someone watching my back."

He took two twenties from his wallet and laid them on the table.

"What's this supposed to be?"

"Just something to help."

"Mo-Mo," she began. It was what she'd called him when they were much younger. "Please, think about it."

That night, Maurice returned home. He would give her the benefit of thinking it over and coming up with ironclad reasons to avoid entering into a business arrangement with her. But the more he thought about it, the more difficult it became to shoot it down. Sitting at the kitchen table, he flipped through bills, loan payments, and overdue notices. He was still in the process of settling his mother's estate, and though she had left him and his sister money, there were already liens against it.

He heard feet on the hardwood floor.

His sister Janice stood there in her pajamas, rubbing her eyes.

"Hey, what are you doing up?"

"I couldn't sleep."

"Why don't you find something good to watch,

I'll be in in a minute."

"Okay."

She was going to be nine in two months. Their mother had been pregnant with her when their father died from an overdose. Maurice flipped through the bills one more time. Felt the weight of them increasing in his hands. He considered Stacy's proposition again. Money had a way of swallowing up principles.

He met her the following day and told her he was willing to get involved.

But, before they could begin, he wanted to do some research, avoid the pitfalls of territorial disputes and extortion. He knew there would be a way to maximize profits and limit their exposure. It would just take some time to figure out.

Stacy moved in to cut down on expenses and share rent.

He mapped out the plan within two weeks.

"Just look," he said when they were seated at the table one night. He had unfolded a map of Charleston across the table.

"There's an untapped resource, right off the highway."

He explained how the trucking industry comprised a majority percentage of the johns who frequented prostitutes in this part of the state. If they kept their operation closer to the interstate, they could capitalize. Not only would they be out on the fringe, away from most of the action, but they could base their enterprise out of his motel.

"I don't know," she said. "Sounds like we've got to cut more people in, or take on another partner."

"I've already put in to switch to the midnight to eight shift." Before she could voice more negative opinions, he continued. "It's right off an exit, sandwiched between a burger joint and a rest stop. It's the perfect location. Also, what are your biggest problems?"

She didn't answer. It was a rhetorical question.

"Protection and the police," he said. "This solves both of 'em.

Stacy paused and took it all in, then slowly nodded. She looked much better now. She was still using, but she'd cut down on the amount and the showers, sleep, and clean clothes did wonders.

She told him she was going to start recruiting talent.

Stacy moved quickly. The following week, she introduced Maurice to Angel and Fantasia. They were tough and weathered, with crudely applied makeup, but they bought into Stacy's pitch. Angel wore purple lipstick and matching eye shadow. Her skin was sallow from some vitamin deficiency. Maurice wondered if she ever saw sunlight.

Fantasia had braces and wore pigtails. Multiple piercings were stuck through each ear. She reminded Maurice of a girl he'd went gone to high school with, which simultaneously aroused and repulsed him. He felt ashamed.

Stacy put everything into motion. They set up in the last room of the motel. Maurice kept two sets of books and logs—one to show the owner, the other to keep track of expenses and income.

Within the first week, they had established their presence. Maurice monitored the cleaning staff to see if they noticed anything out of the ordinary, like why the last room on the ground floor had so much traffic. No one said anything. He was certain they wouldn't be a problem as most of them were in the country illegally.

Everything was going smoothly and word spread. Maurice was stringent about keeping the operation small. He had to remind Stacy that they were making plenty of money already and didn't want to attract the wrong kind of attention.

"No," he said for the third time. They sat around the kitchen table poking at leftovers. Janice was on the couch, and both of them could hear the television keeping her entertained.

"If we keep it small, we don't run unnecessary risks. We can make enough money."

"I'm just saying, maybe we work more shifts, or expand to more rooms."

"We can't."

Although she hemmed and hawed, she ultimately agreed.

After filling the seventh shoe box full of cash, Maurice realized they would need to somehow safe house or launder the money.

Stacy lost count, again.

She looked over at Mo-Mo, who was meticulously keeping the figures in a marbled composition book. She felt the next series of withdrawal symptoms come, and she tried her best not to grimace. Her stomach muscles tightened in on themselves.

He'd only agreed to be her partner if she got clean.

"A junkie won't be able to make on-the-spot moves," he had said. Not to mention, he wouldn't stand for her being high when Janice was around. Stacy gave it a go. She really did. Working a shift kept her mind occupied, and each guy she was with allowed her to think she was one step closer to quitting the life altogether.

They were making good money.

She had a roof over her head and didn't have to

worry about a two-bit hustler with a blade threatening to beat her or, worse, disfiguring her for life.

"You want me to take you to a clinic?" Mo-Mo had asked.

"No, I'll go straight on my own. I promise."

He made like he was going to try to convince her to go to a clinic, but he stopped. So, she'd put down the pills. The first two days were brutal. The withdrawals sent her into pain she didn't think possible. She could have asked to seek treatment, and he would have driven her. He wouldn't have rubbed it in, either—he was always good like that. Maybe, because of the leg braces he had to wear, he never pointed out the shortcomings of others.

No. She wouldn't go, damn it, because she could kick this thing.

By the third day, she could barely get out of bed.

She waited until he went to work. She had been feverish but pumped up the malaise more than was necessary. Quickly, she was out of bed and found the hiding place with her emergency stash. It was still there. Janice was at a neighbor's. Stacy had maybe a forty-minute grace period, which is was all she needed. She dry swallowed three Percocet tablets. The first hit crossed the blood/brain barrier, and she was home.

Instant relief.

This is all I need to do. Just maintain. She could hide it. She had been good at that her whole life.

Eventually, word got back from the girls that some of the truckers didn't like using the motel. Too much exposure. They wanted to remain secure in the cab. The girls argued they could service more people this way. Maurice fought it at first. In the motel, they had the control. Johns would be less prone to start anything if they were in a public place. Stacy and the girls pushed for it, though, and Maurice finally relented.

The first sign of trouble was minor.

Angel came back one night missing a tooth, with a fractured wrist. Some johns liked to get physical, but this was a different animal. Maurice took Angel to the ER, but she would be out of commission for a little while.

They chalked it up to a work-related hazard. Most of the girls were seasoned and although they were pissed, they knew it was part of the game. Still, it bothered Maurice.

"For now, we're under the radar, but, at some point, Vice is going to catch on. We have until then."

He rubbed the bridge of his nose. He felt like he was getting an ulcer. Maybe they *should* expand. Who knew how long their luck would hold out.

Each day, more things had the potential to go wrong. The cops could be turned on to them, or worse, another pimp. This thing with Angel kept him up, though, since it was a problem that couldn't be solved with a payoff.

Another week went by, and things settled down.

Then it happened again. This time, it was Fantasia.

They found her unconscious. Maurice told the doctor he found her by the side of the road, concerned motorist, etc. She had bruised ribs and a concussion. He and Stacy agreed to suspend the business temporarily. When Fantasia was released, she and Angel sat down with Maurice. Didn't take long to realize it was the same guy.

"I don't know, he had blonde hair and a beard."

"And?" Maurice was trying his best not to sound impatient, but this was the third time Angel repeated herself. She looked at him with dead eyes.

"He like wore a hat, too," Fantasia said. She was still somewhat loopy on whatever they'd prescribed, so she was going in and out during their conversation.

"Do you remember what it said?"

Fantasia continued to stare at the ceiling. Her shoulders sank.

"No."

"I gotta get going. I gotta pick up my kid," Angel

said, and lit a Parliament.

"Sure," Maurice said.

"Come on." Angel helped Fantasia up. She winced from the bruises on her chest and sides. When he was alone again, Maurice realized he couldn't handle this problem on his own.

McGill sucked at his teeth. He loved ribs, loved them. But damn it if he didn't always get something caught in his teeth. When it wouldn't dislodge, he grabbed a toothpick from the dispenser.

Across from him, Maurice looked distraught.

"So, how can I help you?"

"Well," Maurice began, but McGill put his hand up. His stomach was rebelling, so he downed some antacid tablets, chased them with a Mickey's, and grimaced until the sensation passed.

"Please," McGill said, making a hand gesture for Maurice to continue.

"We've been having some problems with a john beating up some of the girls."

"I see."

Maurice first came to McGill a little while ago to clean some of his funds. McGill almost choked on his coleslaw when Maurice revealed his profession. The feathered hat and bling was just a movie stereotype, but even so McGill never would have guessed. Maurice was young, too—probably late twenties, early thirties—but there was a quiet, reserved energy about him. He was respectful and spoke with authority.

McGill had driven by the motel once to check it out. Not because he wanted to sample the goods, but he wanted to confirm his suspicions before making arrangements for the kid's funds.

If the operation looked crudely managed, he'd refer the kid to someone else. But everything checked out.

"What do you have in mind?" McGill asked.

Maurice placed the tips of his fingers together to form a pyramid.

"Do you know someone who could stake out this trucker? Maybe put the fear into him?"

McGill sneered and put up his hand. The waiter went through the double doors for entrée number two.

"I happen to know someone."

Gropper got out of the car and stretched his legs. He'd been there for five hours. Nothing so far. That was fine. He had the radio tuned to the jazz station, and they put out a nice mix.

25

He met with McGill three days earlier to hear about the gig. Seemed straightforward enough. Case the place, wait for the action, then settle it. Gropper rolled by two days before and took everything into account.

The process was simple.

The john would approach the girl. She would send him to the front to get a room while she waited. A moment later, the two of them disappeared into the last room on the ground floor. Ten minutes later, the john left, got in his car, and drove away. The girl emerged two minutes after that and stood in the same spot as before, smoking a cigarette.

Gropper made out two other working girls, although it would be difficult to tell if you weren't looking for it. A smart business model. From far away, none of them looked like working girls. They didn't stand around in a group or solicit, they waited to be approached. To anyone keeping surveillance, it looked like a couple getting a room for the evening. Only the one girl continued to use the hotel room. The others were further down, closer to the rest stop. Every so often, another of the girls would return to the room, probably to freshen up or reload for the evening.

Now, on day three, Gropper was finally ready.

He got back into the car and listened to Miles

Davis's *Kind of Blue*. McGill had told him that the two attacks happened a week apart, both within a two-hour window. It made sense that the guy had a route going this way each week, and his pit stop here was his way to relax.

"*We're scanning the scene in the city tonight...*" Larry sang, along with the words to "Seek and Destroy" by Metallica. He had trouble keeping himself contained. He'd been driving for almost twelve hours straight, doing enough crank to keep his teeth sharp, and feeling like if he didn't get some release soon, it would be a problem.

He wasn't a violent person. At least, he didn't consider what he did to be violent. He just lost control, and something else took over. He remembered the last time, still a clear vision in his mind. Her body crumbling before him as if he was were consuming her soul.

Larry liked being on the road. He liked movement. When he was down, if he had any off time, he was just another cog in the wheel. The life suited him. He'd always been an outsider. Sure, he played sports like all the other kids and held his own when challenged, but he took to the solitude. He was king of the road. Most guys burned out. They couldn't handle the stress of the long hours, the boredom, the paralysis. Those were the very things that drew Larry to the trucking life like a moth to a flame. The most rewarding thing, though, was how he had complete freedom.

No house, no car, no kids. No payments due on any of those.

He'd been married earlier in his life. A big mistake. Coming home every night to the same scene. She was a good woman, and they had a nice time for a while. They went to church regularly, had cookouts with the neighbors. She volunteered at the Veterans of Foreign Wars and hosted events for almost every volunteer group.

Larry couldn't put his finger on why, but he began to feel trapped. He withdrew and spent more time away from the house. It had become a prison. She tolerated his behavior at first. They were still newlyweds, and this was probably a natural reaction. But months went by, until it seemed like he was barely there.

They had it out one night. He'd been drinking and came home to an ambush. Before he knew it, his hand flew, depositing her on the floor. She was more shocked than anything, and he was already through the door before she could react. He never went back. He met with her only once more after that, to sign the divorce papers. She could have everything, as far as he was concerned. He went west, as he'd heard most people did when looking for escape.

The trucking company hired him immediately. He had a solid driving record, would work weekends and holidays, and carry any load they asked. Weather wasn't an issue, and he proved he could come in on time. That's all they needed.

Soon, he was making cross-country trips. He learned the ways of the road, picked up the slang, made a vast network of friends who kept him plied with information. After two years on the road, he knew every major thoroughfare through the contiguous states. When asked, Larry could relay information about where to get the cheapest gas, the best sandwiches, or ice cream from a mom-and-pop store. He lived on a diet of coffee, fast food, and speed. Then, of course, there were other needs to be satiated.

Larry had his first encounter two months into his journey.

He'd never had problems before. Transactions went smoothly, he was satisfied, and there were girls aplenty. But this one claimed a different price before they had started. Afterward, she sat with her arms folded and wouldn't leave.

"You said twenty, end of story." Larry held out

the bill.

"Thirty, motherfucker." She wiped at her mouth with a long blue fingernail. Larry nodded. He wondered if this was a racket she threw down on all her clients. She'd stonewall them until they paid her extra. Most guys in his position didn't want trouble, so they were susceptible to shakedowns.

He reached for his wallet, then backhanded her. She fell back against the door in a daze. He leaned over, opened the door, and pushed her out. Her body fell the eight feet, and she landed with a satisfying smack. Larry made sure she'd cleared the tires, then put the truck into gear, and got back on the highway. The euphoria radiated off of him for a full ten minutes afterward. He ruled his kingdom with an iron fist.

Since then, he'd tried so hard not to get violent, but it was difficult to keep the urge under wraps. He knew he'd be pushing his luck if he did it too often. Still, when he did enough crank, and had enough caffeine, it was almost impossible to maintain his composure.

Tonight would be the night.

He discovered the place by the motel almost by accident. He was making trips on I-95 down to Florida. This time, they had him towing cars, two of them piled one on top of the other. It was a small rig, so he could make good time. He pulled into the rest stop, and the girl was standing twenty feet away. Before he knew it, Larry had already rolled down the window and was asking if she wanted to come inside. She extinguished her cigarette, strode over, and took his hand. Inside, she rattled off the business in a somewhat monotone voice.

"What's your name?" Larry said.

"Angel, 'cause baby, I'll make you feel like Heaven."

"Let's get to it," Larry said, unzipping his fly. She took him in her mouth, and he stared straight out the window. He gripped the back of her head, and she tensed up but relented. He felt the familiar buildup, but something was wrong. He squeezed the back of her head and pushed it down. She stopped and pulled back.

"Jesus, not so rough," she said. The fear wasn't in her voice, but the playfulness was gone.

Larry was breathing heavily. He hit her with a closed fist, which caught her on the mouth. It cut his knuckle, and sent one of her teeth flying. Instead of cringing, she cursed and hit him upside the head. He wasn't expecting it, and his ears rang. She tried to hit him again, but he caught her wrist and twisted. She screamed, and he felt her arm give, though the snap wasn't audible. He lunged for her, but his equilibrium was off, and she was able to flee. He drove away quickly, chastising himself for letting things get out of hand. Afterward, he decided he needed to be more careful. He couldn't simply let his urges take over. He'd have to find a new place now when he was in the neighborhood; these girls had guys looking out for them. If Larry or his rig were ever recognized, that would be the end.

However, he found himself on the same stretch of road a week later. He rationalized that he was just being paranoid. The girl was probably an addict. Her encounters with violence were most likely many, and she wouldn't be able to remember anything about him. He was just another john who got out of control. A pitfall of her profession. Not to mention, this was a great setup. He could hide in plain sight along with the other truckers. The highway was right there in case things got hairy.

So, after making sure the same girl wasn't working the corner, he pulled into the rest stop again. This one seemed like a space cadet, and Larry waited until she had begun servicing him, then locked the doors. This time, she couldn't get away. He unloaded all of his pent-up frustration, his rage. When he was finished, he opened the door and let her fall out onto the ground like a jellyfish.

He felt invincible again.

He waited weeks, but now would be the time.

Larry cruised by the rest stop. Neither girl was on the corner. He pulled in and killed the engine. He'd give it ten minutes. If no one came around, he would go into the burger joint, get some food, then call it a night. He'd make his delivery the following day, and he could swing back around on his return trip. Larry reached into the glove compartment and grabbed a pill bottle. He popped some Dexedrine.

He had almost descended from the cab, ready to have his meal, when the girl approached his truck.

For a while, Stacy tried to maintain her appearance. She had been beautiful once. But now, it was a fruitless endeavor. She was also past the point of caring. Maybe some guys out there went for the youthful and naive girl next door, daughter of their business partner, babysitter who needs a ride home. Not the men she worked. They wanted their rocks off. Some requested crazy shit. She had one guy a while back who wanted her to choke him. Others were tame by comparison like the ones who said "Call me 'Big Boy.'"

She'd been out on the streets for almost three years, and she had seen it all. She'd been picked up more than fifty times for solicitation, fought for the opportunity to work a corner. Once, she even ate a meal out of the trash. She'd been humiliated and forced to endure things she'd only read about as cautionary tales.

She dug around her purse.

Stacy carried the essentials for the evening. A mini bottle of Scope and breath mints, her cell phone, and a pint of vodka. She unscrewed the cap and took a quick nip. It burned as always, and she felt a rush of warmth coat the insides of her body. She tugged at her form-fitting dress, pulling it around the curves of her ass.

Her turn to work the rest stop.

Angel was still skittish, so she wanted the room. She had agreed to work even with the cast on her wrist. Fantasia wouldn't be coming back for a while. Stacy felt bad for the others but not too bad. This was life on the streets, what did they think it would be? When she was on her own, she used to carry a switchblade. Soon, she gave it up. It was one thing to get picked up for soliciting or loitering— homicide was another story. She'd been slapped around a few times, so she bought the weapon. She only had it for a month before another girl was charged with attempted murder for sticking a john.

Even if she could plead self-defense, the court

cost alone would bleed her dry. Not to mention every day she wasn't on the street was money she wasn't earning. Stacy ditched the blade. She figured the occasional beating would be the price of doing business. Although, it had rarely come to that. She had a decent sense about her for picking johns. Most were fine, just men with urges, and quick to be done with it. Sometimes, you dealt with some weirdos. Again, part of the gig.

Stacy took another sip. She'd have to pace herself for the rest of the night. She walked to the trash can at the edge of the rest stop and saw the truck idling. It was the first one she'd seen in a while. Odds were it wasn't going to pickup, so she figured she had better make her play before this one took off.

She adjusted her dress one more time, popped a mint, and walked toward the truck.

Gropper sipped his coffee.

He watched the comings and goings of the rest stop, motel, and burger joint. There was only one girl on the corner tonight, so that's where he kept focus. She was tough. Weathered. He figured she had seen her share of things she'd care to forget. Hiding in dumpsters to avoid the cops, and dealing with pimps.

Gropper checked the time.

He'd give it another two hours. The guy had struck between midnight and four, so he probably wasn't going to show after that. Out of the corner of his eye, he saw the girl move. He reached for the Maglite on the passenger seat and hefted it. He wore a black windbreaker and black work pants. To anyone who saw him, he would appear to be a security guard walking the perimeter.

It wasn't the first time the girl had solicited someone this evening, but Gropper wanted to be prepared to leave the car quickly if he had to earn his pay.

The woman adjusted her dress and walk with a focused determination toward the truck. He couldn't make out the driver. For the third time in that evening, Gropper got out of the car. He walked the sixty feet or so and took up his post against the side of the motel. The streetlamps on the corner blazed so brightly that Gropper was cloaked in shadow. It was tough to see into the cab. He debated getting closer, but he didn't want to spook the guy. He'd have to wait and hope to catch something. Then he could act.

* * *

"Hey, man, you got a light?"

The girl was on a break from her shift at the burger joint. She still wore the outfit and held out an unlit cigarette. Larry smiled and pushed in the cigarette lighter.

"Gimme one minute."

He dangled his arm out of the window and swung it back and forth like a pendulum.

"How's it going?" he added.

"Oh, you know."

She was maybe in her late teens or early twenties. She still had acne and the straight teeth of someone who recently gave up their braces or a retainer. Larry imagined what she might be like if he got her into the cab with him, but he chased the thought from his head. Kids didn't do it for him. He'd met all sorts of people on the road, at bars, whore-houses…shit, he even went to a dogfight out in the sticks one time. All types of people in the world, and all of them were into some sort of twisted thing or another. The cigarette lighter popped, and Larry held it for her while she lit her smoke.

"Thanks."

She took a few more drags, extinguished the cig-arette, put the half smoked butt in her shirt pocket, and turned to head back to the restaurant.

"Hey, what's the special tonight?" Larry asked.

37

"I'd stick with the burger," she called out over her shoulder.

A burger did, indeed, sound good.

Stacy liked to imagine she was with Carlos. He had been the captain of the football team, drove a Mustang. He could have had his choice of anyone, but he chose her. She had been someone then.

He'd taken her virginity one night on the middle of the football field. It was cold, but he spread out some blankets. Afterward, they lay together, and he made all sorts of promises. How he would always be there for her, would take her away from this place. They would hop in his car and wouldn't stop driving until they saw the ocean.

He was killed in a drunk driving accident a week later.

That had been almost ten years ago, yet each time she had sex, she imagined the time with Carlos.

The man began praying to God.

Afterward, she rinsed with Scope and spat out the window while he zipped himself up. He wouldn't look at her afterward. Some of them fed off the interaction and condescended to Stacy afterward. Others shrank back from her gaze.

"See you later," Stacy said, opened the door, and

slid down to the ground. As she walked to her spot, she thought she saw something move in the shadows. She waited a moment, but it was gone.

Gropper watched the girl get into the cab. He gripped the Maglite in his left hand. Mentally, he went over a plan. If he had to use it, he'd open the driver's side door with his left, and smash with his right. He watched for another minute, looking for any signs of a struggle, but he soon realized this wasn't their guy.

He would remain where he was, though, just in case.

Gropper's mind wandered. First, he examined the perimeter, then figured out the quickest escape routes. The beauty of the highway system was its unlimited potential to get you far away without being scrutinized. One could be anonymous on the road. He'd made sure to stay moving for a while, as a safety precaution, but at some point, he would need to settle down. The life was beginning to take its toll.

The door to the cabin opened, and instantly Gropper was alert, Maglite ready to shatter bone if need be. It was just the girl. He disappeared further back into the shadows. He felt the wall with his fingertips and followed it around the motel toward his car. He got back inside, killed the rest of his coffee. Another hour went by. Gropper checked the time. Almost four—odds were, their guy wasn't going to show. Gropper turned the key in the ignition, felt the car spring to life, and thought about how wonderful his bed would feel.

Larry walked out of the restaurant and stretched his limbs. The girl was right. The burger was the way to go. He climbed into the cabin. It was only another eight hours or so to Miami. Then he'd get paid, and begin the whole adventure again. The king of the road. He felt his loins stir at the thought of ruling his kingdom. Suddenly, as if ordained as a sacrifice to the one true king, the woman was there. The pose was manufactured, but she was a pro, all right.

He rolled down the window and beckoned her over. She adjusted her dress and walked over to the truck.

"*Scanning the scene in the city tonight*," Larry sang under his breath. He continued to hum as she strolled up. She was much older than he'd thought, but that didn't matter. He was practically bursting at the seams at this point.

"How's it going, baby?" she said.

"Fixing to be better," Larry said. "What'll that cost?"

"Hands twenty, mouth forty. We can negotiate from there."

Larry produced two twenties and handed them out the window. He watched her take the money and put it on a roll, then tuck it into her purse. She signaled back to the motel, then walked around to the passenger side and climbed up. She placed her bag on the floor.

"Let me see 'em," Larry said.

"Sure, baby," she said and unzipped the front of her dress. She reached in and brought out two breasts losing the fight with gravity. The word *Carlos* had been tattooed crudely over her heart. She positioned herself and undid Larry's belt buckle. He reclined in the seat as she worked. He didn't register anything for a moment, blinded as he was by the change taking hold of him. He gripped the back of her head and guided her quicker.

Stacy was on the ball field again. She could feel the cool night air prickle her skin. When she looked up, the night's sky was a scattershot of stars. Carlos had placed his hand on the back of her head. The euphoria was suddenly cut short by Carlos squeezing the back of her neck. The memory broken, she tried to reel back, but the trucker's hand remained firm. She gagged, and he let her go.

Immediately, she sensed trouble and somehow knew this was the guy. He had a far-off look in his eyes. She had seen it before in men who became violent quickly. She did her best to maintain her composure.

"Easy, baby," she said. "If you want to get rough, it's going to cost you more."

He glanced toward his wallet in an automatic response, and she swung for him. She was in an awkward position, but her punch connected on his cheek. His head snapped back, and she made a play for the door.

Larry sat there more stunned than anything else. Rage overtook him.

"You!" was all he managed to get out. She had gotten the door open when he grabbed the back of her dress and pulled her back. In close quarters it was hard to maneuver, but he pinned her down on her back with his left hand and closed the door with his right.

"Oh, you fucked up," Larry said.

He threw an elbow once, which hit her in the forehead. She didn't cry or scream like the others.

This one seemed to understand. He almost admired her for that. The second elbow split her eyebrow, and blood flowed down her face. She moaned, and he took a breath. Why rush? He could take his time with this one as he felt she deserved it. Hadn't she asked for it? Larry locked the doors and ran his fingers through his hair. He felt his cheek where she landed her shot. It would probably bruise, but if he iced it later, maybe it wouldn't show.

Larry spun in his seat and lifted his right leg to stomp her. He brought it down with a satisfying crunch. He was going for a second shot when the driver's side window shattered.

Gropper didn't like to carry weapons. Some in his line of work preferred weighted gloves, a sap, or an expandable baton. They could be concealed and inflict a lot of damage if used properly, though still be nonlethal. But if you got picked up with one, it automatically placed you under suspicion. Besides, anything could become a weapon in the proper hands. Over time, he'd learned how to use everything at his disposal. Similarly, he'd picked up techniques that he could incorporate. Some martial arts were better than others, and he learned how to apply them to any given situation, be it close quarters or on the ground. He never liked to engage without a tactical advantage. This wasn't a dojo. No rules or showing respect to your opponent.

It was kill or be killed.

Gropper shattered the window using a window punch—a small device mainly used by first responders for victims in car crashes. The tip had three small prongs placed against the window. When triggered, the bolt shot out with enough PSI to collapse the window. The whole thing was less then than three inches in length, retailed for less than ten bucks, and served as Gropper's key ring. If anyone searched him, they would write it off as him just being a cautious person.

The trucker inside flinched and protected his face as best he could.

Gropper knocked the remnants of the tempered glass loose, gripped the guy's collar, and pulled the guy through the now- open window. The guy fell to the ground with a solid thud and was stunned. Gropper picked him up. The guy was disoriented. He threw a haymaker, which Gropper blocked with the Maglite. Then, in the same motion, he hit the guy solidly in the liver with the flashlight. The trucker wheezed and fell backward on his butt.

Gropper helped him up again and walked him to the side of the motel. They continued past the motel into the rear parking lot and arrived at Gropper's car. Gropper hit the guy once in the kidney with the Maglite, and the man bellowed, then fell over. He retched once, dry heaving onto the ground. Gropper popped the trunk, hit the guy a final time on the head, and the man was out cold. He flipped him into the trunk, then duct taped his ankles and wrists and placed a hood on his head. He shut the trunk and waited. A few moments went by. He turned slowly and studied the parking lot. Nothing. At this time of night, everyone was asleep or on the road.

Gropper went back to the truck. He saw the girl outside of the cab clutching at her head. She hadn't seen him, so he stayed back. As long as she was up and moving, he wasn't concerned. She'd live. She had enough seasoning to know how to handle a situation like this. Gropper watched her walk toward the burger joint. She'd call for a cab and head to the hospital, tell them some story of being attacked. She didn't have any bullet or knife wounds, so they wouldn't call the police. Whether they bought it was a different story, but again, it made no difference to Gropper.

He returned to the car. He could hear the guy in the trunk shifting around. Must be on some sort of amphetamine or something. Gropper put the car in gear and pulled out.

* * *

Larry's stomach felt like it was on fire.

He didn't know how long he'd been in the trunk. He started flailing when he came to, but realized he needed to keep his strength. The guy was probably the girl's pimp out for some revenge. The car finally came to a stop. Larry heard the guy get out of the car, and the trunk opened. A beat. Then the guy spoke.

"You're going to get a series of instructions, one at a time. Do you understand?"

"Yes." Larry's voice croaked out from between cracked and dried lips.

He felt pressure on his ankles, and the duct tape gave way.

"Climb out."

Larry hesitated for a moment, then felt for the edge with his leg. He sat back on his butt and swung both legs out. He angled to the left and stood up. Early morning sounds drifted through the silence.

"Forget about this place. Forget about these girls."

"I know, I will. I promise."

Larry was desperate. The man had kept the hood on him, which could only mean something truly awful. But the guy contradicted that thought with his warning. It was about the girls. Sure, he could stay away. There were plenty of them he could visit.

"Whatever you want," Larry added.

Silence.

"What?" Larry asked. He had trouble keeping his voice level.

"They thought you should have a reminder."

Gropper saw the man shake. He hit the guy twice in the chest with the Maglite, breaking both of his collarbones. The guy grunted and buckled a few times, then Gropper pushed him to the ground. He took the Maglite to the guy's hip bones. He wasn't sure he'd broken them, but there was a hell of a crunch upon impact. The guy was hyperventilating. The hood was inflating and deflating rapidly. Gropper used the razor on his window punch to cut the rest of the duct tape around the guy's wrists. He rolled the guy on his stomach, removed the hood, got in the car, and drove away.

They were in the parking lot of a hospital. At some point, someone would find the trucker. Either that, or he'd drag himself to the emergency room. Gropper didn't care what happened.

His message had been received, loud and clear.

* * *

Gropper pulled into his spot. The sun had just crept out, and rays covered the quiet neighborhood. He got out and surveyed the block. John wasn't there, but he never worried about this time of day. Gropper crossed the street, got to his door, undid the police lock, and stepped inside.

He was still jazzed with adrenaline, so he opened the inner door to head to the kitchen. Ms. Bradley kept a fifth of Evan Williams in the pantry. Gropper poured himself half a glass with ice. It was quiet. A stillness always on the verge of being shattered. Gropper heard a creaking noise that kept repeating. He walked toward the front door and found it open, but the screen door closed. Peering out the threshold, he found Ms. Bradley sitting in her rocking chair on the front porch.

Slowly, she rocked back and forth, a peaceful look upon her face.

Gropper opened the screen door, and she looked toward him. She smiled, and he moved to join her on a neighboring chair. They sat together in silence while Gropper sipped his drink.

"I do love to see the sunrise," Ms. Bradley said.

She was cocooned in a blanket and spoke with the eloquence of a woman with a proper education.

She glanced over at Gropper, her eyes glazed from sleep and whichever combination of prescription drugs she'd been taking. Gropper wondered how many sunrises she would have in the future. She'd buried her husband years ago, but unlike many who can't cope with the loss of a spouse, she stayed active and part of the community. Now age had finally caught up.

She shut her eyes.

They sat together for a little while longer, until the humidity set in and sweat beaded on her forehead. She started to rise from her chair with difficulty. Gropper was already up and standing next to her.

"Let me help you," he said.

He could sense that in years gone by, she would have turned down the courtesy, but now, in her condition, she welcomed the help. Gropper slid his arm under the bend of her knees and the other around her back. He lifted her as if she was nothing.

"Oh, my," she said.

Gropper turned and walked to the screen door and opened it with his heel. He carried her up the stairs and placed her back in her bed. He returned downstairs, poured her a glass of milk, and left it on her end table.

"Thank you," she said.

Gropper nodded and returned to the porch. He killed his drink, went back inside, and secured the front door. He got into his own bed and stared at the ceiling for a moment, trying to decipher if there were any patterns in the chipping paint.

Maurice sat across from McGill and wondered if the man ever left the diner. Did they charge him rent? Did they give him everything on the house in exchange for his services? Did McGill actually own the joint? More importantly, how the hell had he not had a heart attack?

He watched McGill shovel in a fistful of fries with gravy, and his own stomach turned.

Maurice had looked over the laminated menu, but he didn't have an appetite. McGill finished his food, wiped his hands on his napkin, and signaled the waiter for more coffee.

"So," McGill said, "problem solved."

Maurice felt the weight lift off his shoulders.

"Thank God."

"This guy won't be bothering anyone for a while. Shit, this guy's not going to be doing much of anything for a while." McGill laughed and dipped some more fries in a pool of ketchup and then mayonnaise.

Maurice just nodded. He didn't press McGill for the details. He sat back and opened the menu. Stacy's wounds were mostly superficial, and she would recover quickly. If McGill's guy hadn't gotten there, the trucker might have killed her.

Stacy called him after she'd been assaulted, and Maurice met her at the hospital. He pulled up, and she was already waiting for him outside. She had a butterfly bandage on her eyebrow, and one eye was closed from the swelling. Purple and yellow blotches decorated her cheek.

"Are you okay?" he asked when she slid into the passenger seat.

"I'm fine. Can we go?"

Maurice stared at her for a moment, then put the car in gear. They didn't speak for the rest of the ride home. Maurice started to say something a few times, but when he looked at her, he could tell she didn't want to hear anything.

The car came to a stop outside of their apartment, and she finally spoke.

"This is what happens, okay? If you want me to release you of any guilt or blame, consider it done."

Maurice remained silent.

When they went inside, he spent some time looking through his finances. He told her that as soon as he'd made enough money to cover his outstanding debts, he would dissolve their partnership.

She had agreed.

Now he sat in the booth more relieved than anything else. They would be out of business for a little while until the girls healed up, but soon enough, though, they would be operational, and he could wash his hands of this entire thing.

His appetite returned.

He ordered pancakes and a side of bacon.

McGill watched Maurice leave. His schedule was clear for the rest of the day, but he wouldn't leave the diner for another few hours. Business always had a way of finding him, and he made it easy to be found. McGill never liked to carry a phone on him. He was still old school. He used a beeper and the pay phone in back near the toilets.

At one point, the owner had planned to get rid of it and put in a gumball machine or something, but McGill persuaded him to keep it. For his favorite customer, the owner acquiesced. The staff had been instructed to find McGill if that phone rang. No one ever questioned the owner about the man who rarely left the back booth.

That morning, McGill's pager had buzzed. The coded message from Gropper: Everything went off without a hitch. McGill could always count on Gropper to deliver. He was McGill's best asset. Once, as a test, he put a few guys on Gropper to see what they'd come up with. All three of them were made within the first hour.

McGill finished his coffee and began on the pecan pie.

Another day, another dollar.

Gropper was sitting in the living room listening to "Blue in Green." He'd been able to escape to the far reaches of solace when a buzzing sound broke him from his trance. He couldn't place it at first, but felt the familiar vibration of the pager.

Gropper lifted the needle off the record.

He drove to a strip mall nearby, went to the bank of pay phones, and dialed McGill. The man picked up on the first ring—not a good sign. In all the time they had done business together, even if things were important, McGill always had to be summoned from his booth.

"Yeah," Gropper said.

"We have a problem," McGill said. "See you soon."

McGill hung up.

Gropper was in the booth within fifteen minutes.

McGill hadn't eaten anything.

"The trucker you laid out."

"Yeah?"

"Is there any way he can ID you or your car?"

"Not possible."

"I didn't think so." McGill paused. "The guy's on the mend right now at MUSC, but the cops will be headed there soon."

"What's going on?"

"It'll hit the news tonight. I got it from one of my guys. They seized a hundred and fifty kilos of uncut cocaine from the trunk of one of the cars your guy was hauling."

McGill relayed the rest of what he knew.

The truck had stayed there for an entire day. When no one claimed it the day after that, the owner of the burger jointed had it towed. The truck went to the police impound and was inspected. They found a legitimate bill of lading for the car, as well as registration for the company. The trunk of the car was the last thing they opened.

It was the biggest single narcotics seizure in the last ten years. Eventually, it would become lore, the punchline of jokes. There was mass speculation about the true owners.

"It'll make the national in an hour."

Gropper nodded.

The news report would be the least of their problems. The cops would find the trucker pretty quickly, but again, it would be a dead end. They would sniff around for a little while, but the bust would satisfy any pressure the department may have been facing. They would be happy enough to let it go.

The true owners of the cocaine, however, would not.

"What's the play?" McGill took a huge bite of a burger with bacon, cheddar cheese, sour cream, and avocado.

Gropper thought about it. If this thing came down, it might not ever get to them. He'd taken out the trucker clean. No one knew who he was. But McGill had more dealings in play.

"How far are you willing to go?" Gropper said.

He watched McGill decide, take another bite of his burger, slowly chew, and then swallow.

"Let's take it one step at a time."

"All right. The trucker."

Hector sat in a terry cloth robe now in a chair on the balcony of his high-rise apartment overlooking Miami Beach. The sun was still an hour or two from setting, painting the beach in alternating shades of orange and purple. He took a sip of his wine. The bottle cost more than most people made in six months.

He didn't immediately worry about his safety. He had made himself too important to the organization. *Be value added*, he had learned. No matter what, make people think you're worth more with them than against.

Hector was a logistics man.

Others before him built the empire. Miami had been a hotbed of activity for drugs. A major importing hub, first marijuana, then cocaine. More than half of the infrastructure, roads, buildings, all built from the revenue of the drug trade. However, the desire to abuse drugs never went away.

Soon, the empire was resurrected, albeit with different leaders, and business went on as usual.

Hector got up and walked over to the balcony railing. The phone call had ruined what he hoped would be a great day. Now, of course, it had been soured, and he was tasked with repairing the situation.

Hector closed his eyes and smelled the sea air.

He grew up in Miami, went to school and college there. He studied accounting. He approached some connected men, through a college contact, and was brought in to handle some of the books. One of his innovative ideas: Pack the shipment in the trunk of a car, then have the car towed. The driver wouldn't know anything about it, and if he got pulled over or busted, he would have plausible deniability.

He had explained the risks, of course, as nothing was foolproof.

The key was to limit their exposure as well as diversify their method of transportation. They would have an air-drop coming up from Colombia, mule things in by commercial flight and boat, with multiple cars towed coming from up north. No one would suspect anything from up north. Hector had listened to his predecessors mention these tactics, and he didn't forget.

He'd receive the car, and the product, and safe house them until one of the distributors showed up. It had been a good system.

Hector had been called yesterday by the foreman at the garage. One of the deliveries was still outstanding. This in and of itself was nothing to be worried about. Many factors could delay the truck's arrival. Hector learned over the years to keep his reactions measured and his anxiety under control. It all fell under his precept of being value added. Someone who acted out, couldn't maintain his composure, this was someone who would not last long in a business where death was the answer to problems without hesitation.

The most recent phone call, though—that was troublesome.

The police in South Carolina had their product. Again, this did not worry Hector's superiors. While they were upset at their misfortune, they understood this was the price of doing business. Dealers would lose counts, money would be siphoned, drugs would be consumed by people working for them. These were all agreed-upon aspects of the game. It would be suspect if these things didn't happen. However, what concerned Hector's bosses was whether this was the work of their enemies, or even worse, an inside job.

The instructions had been brief but thorough.

Since the seizure of their drugs had happened under Hector's watch, he had to make it right. He needed to investigate and report back to them.

He opened the sliding door and walked back into the air-conditioned living room. It was almost entirely see-through glass, giving a panoramic view of downtown Miami. He sat down at the table.

Luz was on the couch in a bikini, watching a reality television program about fixing old houses.

"Are you finally ready?" she asked.

She had been pestering him to go to the beach for the last forty minutes. He told her he needed to clear his mind for a little.

"That's what the beach is for," she told him.

He smiled.

"I just need to think some things through, alone."

She turned over on the couch allowing him to see her full figure.

"Okay, half an hour," he said.

"Fine." She fell back onto the couch and began channel surfing.

He turned and looked at her. She lay on her side. She easily could have been a swimsuit model for any of the catalogs. He had picked her up a few weeks ago on South Beach, spotted her with a few friends. He told the man with the earpiece to round them all up and part the velvet ropes. That's all it took. She never asked what he did for a living, as long as she had the trappings of luxury.

"A few more minutes, I promise." He tried to sound sincere.

He turned on his computer and heard the shifting on the couch, then the soft footfalls as she approached him. Luz put her hands on his shoulders and began massaging them.

"That's nice," he said.

She slid her hands across his chest and down to his stomach.

"Or, we could stay here for a while longer."

* * *

The best *bistec de palomilla* in Miami wasn't found in a five-star restaurant. It was in a small, family-owned place in Little Havana. Ermano had discovered it by accident. He tore into the meat as an animal would after starving for a few days. He leaned back in his chair to take a breath and listened half-heartedly to the two men at a nearby table talk about politics. They were discussing everything from gun control to censorship.

He laughed.

They knew nothing of how things really worked. It was impossible to know unless you had been chewed up and spit out by the machine.

Ermano grew up in Cuba. He'd gotten into trouble as soon as he could walk. He was already imprisoned by the time he was sixteen. Prison sharpened him like a knife. After his first year on the inside, he was already carrying out hits. People feared him, and he acquired the nickname *La Espada*, The Blade, since his weapon of choice was a machete. Eventually, he got a job in the prison infirmary and learned how to be a more effective and subtle killer. Ermano left a trail of bodies during his tenure in prison. Then, in 1980, Castro opened the prisons and sent most of the hardened criminals to the

United States during the Mariel Harbor boatlift.

It was easy for him to find work in the US.

People needed labor. Syndicates needed assassins. Though his best years were behind him, it also gave him the perfect cover. No one suspected that a man of advanced age would be the one to take his life. Ermano kept himself in good shape. He could do five hundred push-ups without stopping, and he could crush an apple with his bare hand. During the day, he performed landscaping duties and kept a low profile.

He disposed of people when needed. Thoughts of retirement crossed his mind from time to time, spending more time with his grandchildren. But he always pushed them aside. Taking the life of another, the feeling of being judge, jury, executioner—he couldn't pass it up.

His cell phone rang. Hector.

"*Hola.*"

"*La mano que maneja el cuchillo,*" Hector said. He spoke a coded message for about a minute. Ermano hung up and returned to his steak.

The men had grown loud now from too much drinking. They were arguing about Guantanamo and due process. Ermano envisioned himself rising, getting his machete from the van, and going to work on the them. Maybe he'd start at the ankles on one and the wrists on the other. He'd explain to them how it was all an illusion. Once a little pressure was applied, rules and order went out the window. People tasted pain, and they would compromise their beliefs. He thought about hordes of men who pleaded with him to make the torture stop. He usually hadn't even gotten started at that point. He enjoyed his work. A man who does not enjoy what he does lacks purpose in life.

Suddenly, the men laughed, and Ermano gripped his cutlery until his knuckles turned white. He relaxed and forked another piece of steak into his mouth.

He would channel his fury tomorrow.

Larry stared at the nurse's cleavage. He figured he was allowed after the hell he'd been put through. She spooned some more pudding and some of it fell down his chin.

"Oops," she said, and wiped it off, which meant she had to lean forward.

It didn't matter that she was a good forty pounds overweight and could use a few hours at a salon. That didn't bother him at all. She finished giving him his dessert, made sure his water and straw combo was in reach, and left him for the night.

Larry sat back in his hospital bed.

He knew he should be happy to be alive. He was initially. Then he began crawling toward the hospital. The pain was so excruciating that he passed out. They had hooked him up to something called a PCA machine. He could dispense painkillers at the push of the green button. Just enough to take the edge off.

Larry tried to shift. He had to be careful. Major movements still caused his teeth to chatter from pain.

He was in a contraption that kept his shoulders pulled back. He had a cast like a chastity belt that went from his stomach down to his knees. Thank God he wouldn't have to shit in a bag permanently. Slowly, he inched backward, with minor discomfort. He rested his head, then pressed the button to raise the bed.

The police had stopped by to see if he wanted to fill out an incident report. He told them he didn't remember anything. Said there might have been four or five opponents for all he knew, but it felt like baseball bats were hitting him.

One of them left a card just in case Larry thought of anything.

Shit, he wouldn't have told them anything anyway. No need to get involved with a psychopath's vendetta. Larry sensed that as long as he stayed out of this neck of the woods, he would be fine. There was plenty of open territory on the road. He could collect disability for the short term, plus some workers' comp. A lesser man would want to sue anyone and everyone possible, but Larry just wanted to get back out on the road. He was beginning to feel cooped up in this room. He had a neighbor who'd been discharged earlier in the day, so it was nice to be alone. But, he knew that wouldn't last.

He pressed the button. Soon he'd get another dose.

Ermano drove all night. He knew they were on a deadline. The cops would check the registration and track down their guy to the hospital. The trucker wouldn't know anything, of course, and the company had just been filling an order. If anything, the police would find dead ends. Still, you never wanted to leave anything to chance. Plus, they needed some information before the police meddled too much.

Ermano pulled into the hospital parking lot.

The beauty of driving a landscaping truck meant you were above suspicion. Ermano got out and stretched his legs. Long rides wore on his body, and although he was in good shape, you can't fight against age and time.

Ermano took the phone from his pocket and pushed a button to dial a stored number.

"*Estoy aquí,*" he said.

The man on the other end of the phone was one of a dozen or so tech experts the syndicate had on payroll. He read off the trucker's name, his room, his diagnosis, the layout of the floor, and when the nurses were most likely to do their rounds. Ermano listened patiently, then hung up. He grabbed the bag of supplies from the glove compartment.

He shut his eyes and let everything settle into place before he walked to the hospital.

He found the main entrance and waited. He wanted to make sure the nurses had finished their shifts checking on patients and administering meds.

He could easily pass for a custodial worker, but he didn't have to worry about cameras, since HIPAA would prevent them from being used. Hospitals were designed to be responsive to emergencies, not preventative.

Ermano walked in through the front door.

Larry felt a presence near his bed, and he opened his eyes. He was hoping maybe it was a nurse with a sponge bath. Instead, he saw a man in overalls.

The guy was old, Latino, maybe the janitor. Larry tried to speak, but he felt like his tongue was covered in cement. His eyelids were weighted down and closed on him without his permission.

"What happened to you?" the man said.

Larry fought to regain consciousness and regaled the man with everything that happened to him, from pulling in to the burger joint, to being accosted by either a thief or pimp, and coming here. He even mentioned the police who interviewed him.

"Nothing about the drugs?" the man said.

"Drugs?"

"Good. Thank you, my friend. Get some rest."

The man left the room, and Larry tried to keep his head afloat. *Jesus Christ.* He felt a surge of something more powerful take hold and render him mute. It burned like white fire. He stared up at the ceiling as it opened and light shone down upon him as if it was Judgement Day.

Ermano departed as fast as possible from the room before the man's coding vital signs were to alert the staff. He took the stairs down to the lobby and grabbed a Coke from the vending machine near the front. He learned over the years to hide in plain sight. A man moving quickly has eyes drawn to

him. A man pausing to drink a soda, no one paid
attention to. He walked through the sliding glass
doors, surveyed the parking lot, and saw no one.
Still too early in the morning. He took another sip
of Coke, dumped the remnants of the liquid in the
trash by the entrance, then slipped the used syringe
inside the can.

Odds were, the trucker's heart would have
stopped by now. He'd given the man barbiturates
to loosen his tongue and keep him passive. Once he
got the information he came for, he shot the man
up with potassium.

Ermano threw the can in the trash and went to
his truck. Too early in the morning for any of the
prostitutes to be out. He checked his watch. They
probably wouldn't start their stroll for another sixteen hours. Ermano figured he would check into the
motel near where they worked and get a few hours
of shut-eye.

Always sleep when you can.

The phone rang, and a waitress grabbed it.

"McGill," Gropper said. He waited. He could
hear the phone bang against the wall as it dangled.

"Shit," he heard McGill say in the background,
then some rustling.

"Yeah."

"The trucker's dead. Heart attack."

Gropper listened while McGill processed the information.

"What do you think?"

"They move fast. We've got to imagine they know what we know."

"Jesus." McGill sighed. "You know, you try to help some people."

Gropper waited.

"Think they'll hit the motel?" McGill asked.

"If they're not already there."

"All right. See if you can take care of this without any collateral damage. But if it comes down to it, nothing comes back to me."

"You got it."

Gropper hung up the pay phone. He was at the bus station. Midday, the place was empty. He walked through the central terminal toward a bank of lockers. He found his, inserted the key, and opened it. Removing the gym bag, he shut the locker behind him and settled in a form-fitting blue seat near the corner. He checked the contents. He had about five grand in cash, a passport, a snub-nosed .22, a Karambit knife, and a travel toiletry kit. He carried the bag to the car, put it in the trunk, and got into the driver's seat.

He shut his eyes and sat in silence.

Gropper remembered reading about the Stoics during his travels—philosophers who held that a virtuous person, who sticks to their beliefs, is unassailable by the outcomes of their actions.

He drove to his house.

Getting out of the car, he spotted John, who wiped his nose.

Gropper raised his hand in acknowledgment and made his way to the side door. Inside, he found Ms. Bradley in the living room listening to her records.

"Hello," she said.

"How are you feeling?"

"Tired. I seem to get so tired these days."

"Get some rest."

Gropper sat down in one of the empty chairs, and they listened to Wes Montgomery. Together, they remained in silence until Gropper noticed she had fallen asleep. He picked her up and carried her upstairs to bed. The courtesy shuttle would be by in a little to help her to the hospital.

Gropper placed his hand on her forehead.

He held it there for a moment, then went downstairs, removed the record, and put it back on the shelf. He went through the efforts of wiping down his room for fingerprints. He removed the clothes from the armoire and his second bag from the foot of the bed and took everything out to the car.

Gropper looked around for a moment, then got in and drove away.

The door opened, and the little bell rang. Maurice hated that bell more than anything. As a result, he had developed an automatic response anytime the door opened. People checking in weren't bad. It was people coming to complain about noise in neighboring rooms, or the hot water pressure, or the fucking ice wasn't cold enough in the ice dispensary. Not to mention, he was still having stomach trouble due to the stress of the recent events. Thank God, they were over, but they still weighed on him.

He looked up and saw the elderly Latino man. Maurice slipped into his business persona.

"How can I help you?"

The man walked to the edge of the desk.

"That place any good?" he asked, and tilted his head in the direction of the burger joint.

"It's not bad."

"Ah, the opposite." The man smiled and plucked one of the wrapped mints from a bowl on the counter.

"It's probably better than you'll find in the immediate area, unless you want to drive."

"No, thanks. Too much driving already. Just need to sit for a while."

"Well, here's a coupon. We have a deal with them."

"*Gracias*," the man said.

Maurice nodded, hoping this would conclude their conversation.

The man pocketed the coupon, opened the wrapper, and popped the mint into his mouth.

"Listen, if someone wanted some action, where would they go?"

"Action?" Maurice tried to keep the surprise out of his voice.

"Yeah, you know? Music? Movies?"

"Oh, well, there's a multiplex nearby, and in the next strip mall there's a bar that does live music."

"Thanks again." The man cracked the mint in between his teeth and walked out.

The bell rang at his departure and Maurice groaned at the sound.

The man at the desk was in on it, that much was clear to Ermano. The eyes had given him away when he reacted to the word "action." He couldn't have been the one to take out the trucker, so there had to be a third player. The desk man was probably on some sort of a payoff.

Ermano went to his truck. He pulled the phone from the glove compartment and dialed a number. Hector picked up.

Ermano gave him a report of his activities over the last few hours, including the trucker's interrogation and disposal, as well as the encounter with the desk man at the motel.

"So, this isn't sabotage?" Hector said.

"No, no one is making a move against you."

"Well, in that case, take whatever measures you see fit to end this."

"*Sí.*"

Ermano put the phone in his pocket for any trophy pictures later. He had arrived at the best part of any job, when his handlers cut him loose and allowed him to do what he did best. He would wait for the cover of nightfall, then descend on them like a plague.

Maurice got to his car and laid his crutches against the back door. He fumbled for the keys in his pocket and dropped them. He saw the shadow coming toward him, then he was out cold. He awoke again, and he was in the driver's seat.

"Just listen," the person said from the back.

Maurice didn't say anything. The guy who'd been in earlier, looking for action. He felt the man's left hand on his shoulder. It squeezed just enough to demonstrate the man's strength. Maurice flinched a little from the pressure.

"Don't do anything at all. We're just going to sit here for a moment while I talk. You may speak."

"Okay," Maurice said.

"I'm looking for a person of considerable skill who beat up a trucker here recently."

"I don't know what you're talking about."

The man squeezed again, and this time Maurice felt pain.

"I went through someone, alright? I don't know the guy."

"Good, we're getting somewhere." The man relaxed his grip.

"Now," the man continued. "Drive around to the room you've been using. You're going to contact this person."

The phone rang, and McGill didn't wait for someone to get it. He had trouble wedging himself out of the booth at first, and vowed he would eat more greens, but he was at the phone by the fourth ring.

"Yeah."

"Hey, it's Maurice, there's someone here."

The phone went dead.

McGill hung up the phone. He walked back to his table. If they had gotten to Maurice, then they could get to him. Unless Gropper was as good as McGill thought. He returned to the table, spread butter on the pancakes and bacon, then poured the syrup.

He took the first bite and chased it with Mickey's.

They could come for him. He was a survivor, after all. Or, he could go somewhere else and set up shop. Although, he doubted he'd be able to find a better diner than this.

Ermano stood before them. Two girls were gagged, their hands and feet tied with sheets. They shook and cried, though it was muffled by the fabric. They kept trying to scream, but it was futile. The man from the front desk sat on the edge of the bed by the phone. He seemed haunted, as if he'd known this day was coming and was resigned to it.

"What now?" he asked.

"Well..."

Ermano sat down on the bed. He put his arm around the young man. He could feel the kid's heart beating through his back.

"What's your name?"

"Maurice."

"What do you think will happen?"

Maurice looked back at the girls on the ground, then he turned and stared at Ermano. Perhaps he wasn't resigned, as there was fire there still. Ermano was impressed. He had put many people—perceived tough guys, capos, stone cold killers—in the same position, and those men could not maintain the same eye contact.

"You needed us to serve a purpose, and now the purpose is over, so we're expendable." Maurice licked his lips like he was getting the up his nerve.

"However, if you kill all of us, then it becomes a multiple homicide, which raises a bunch of questions. Plus, if you leave the state, you can forget police, we're talking FBI. I don't think you want to have to deal with that scenario. We're all doing something illegal, so you can believe me when I tell you, we won't say anything. After all, you want the guy who took out your associate."

Ermano started to laugh.

Perhaps he'd underestimated this kid.

"You've got some *huevos*, I'll give you that," Ermano said. He patted Maurice on the back a few times.

Ermano reached to his belt buckle. It was an

ornate silver thing with intricate etching in the shape of a bull's head. Both ends concealed push knives. He gripped the kid by the back of his shirt. His right hand shot for one of the handles and hit the kid in the stomach three times. Maurice hunched over, and his eyes practically bulged from their sockets. Ermano flung him back onto the bedspread.

"You've no business in this world."

Maurice gripped at his stomach while blood seeped around his hands and crimson soon engulfed flesh. The girls started to convulse and slide on the ground like slugs when their cover has been removed.

Ermano cocked his head to the side. He felt the familiar rush in his chest, and he approached them with renewed force.

"Shhhh," Ermano said. "This is all going to be over soon."

Stacy needed to use the bathroom, and she hated using the bathroom at the truck stop. The burger place wouldn't let her use theirs unless she was a paying customer, and she'd be damned if she was going to buy a drink just to use the toilet.

She walked out farther into the parking lot, to get a better vantage point, and saw the light was on in the room. Who knew if they had someone in there—that was the last thing she needed, interrupting Angel during a session, she'd never hear the end of it.

Stacy walked back to her spot.

Fuck it, she thought and headed toward the motel.

Ermano had trouble calming down. The lizard part of his brain had overtaken him, and the fury still coursed through him. He flung the second girl's body to the ground. He wiped the sweat from his brow. His enemy would come soon, then Ermano would finish the job and head home. The desk kid was smart, but he didn't know shit.

Ermano wiped his forehead on his sleeve. The room smelled raw and feral, with the overpowering scent of copper. He calmed his breathing.

The man would probably burst into the room shooting. Ermano would wait by the door, then he'd get him.

Ermano wiped more blood from his face and walked toward the entrance.

The knife shot out from under the bed and into his foot. Ermano didn't even feel it at first, then toppled forward as an incredible pain flew up his leg.

* * *

Nothing comes back to me, McGill had said.

No loose ends.

Gropper knew he'd see the faces of the girls in his sleep for a long time. Wide-eyed, they were pleading with him. Faces fixed in the extreme terror of those who know their end is coming soon. He looked away, so he wouldn't have to see them. He heard the muted conversation taking place above him.

The kid trying to buy time, to prolong his life for a few more moments. Gropper knew he was dead before he began speaking. Then, the Latino laughed, the sudden shift and creaking of bed springs. Gropper felt the tremors of the knife sticking the kid. He heard his labored breathing as the life bled out of him. Then the Latino moved from the bed and addressed the girls.

He was a pro, but he was clearly a psychopath. So, Gropper would wait until he was in full transformation. Then the guy might be more prone to making a mistake. Gropper watched the first girl be plucked from the floor, then heard her get tenderized with the push knife. She thudded against the wall, and her feet tap-danced against the floor, while the man held her in the air. He was strong and full of adrenaline.

Gropper took the folding Karambit knife, opened it, and waited. It was a curved blade, like a crescent, and Gropper had honed the edge.

The man continued his assault on the second girl until well after she was dead. Gropper watched her feet shake and then go slack. The man threw her to the ground with more ardor than before. The man's breathing was audible. He crossed by the bed, and Gropper sliced his foot. The man grunted and fell forward. Gropper rolled out from under the bed.

He turned, and they faced each other. The man started laughing and reached down to remove a second push knife from his belt buckle. He came forward, putting weight on his bad foot, and stumbled. Gropper lunged with his own blade and swung twice, missing the first time, but slicing the man's forearm on the second attempt. The man gritted his teeth, dropped a knife, and let fly an expletive before backing away to regroup.

Gropper didn't give him any quarter.

He moved forward. Even at an advanced age, the man struck with complex balletic moves. The first one missed, the second cut Gropper on his forehead. He reset himself. They were both breathing heavily now, and he knew fights like these would deteriorate soon to less finesse and more blunt attacks.

The man feinted with a shot and blocked Gropper's attack. He stuck Gropper in the stomach. He ripped the knife up, expecting Gropper to wither and drop. Instead, the man's look of victory faded as Gropper stuck him between the ribs. Gropper twisted the knife, and the man's face imploded. He gurgled forth a breath. Gropper dropped the body on the ground and placed his Karambit in the hands of one of the prostitutes.

Gropper turned just in time to see the flash go off.

The man smiled and held the phone outstretched as his thumb maneuvered along the screen.

"*Buena suerte*," the man said, then the light left his eyes. Gropper took the phone from the man's hand and pocketed it.

He took off his shirt, removed the duct tape, and sliced phone book from his stomach. He took off his surgical gloves and placed everything in a garbage bag. Once outside, he threw the garbage bag in the trunk and got in the car. He caught his breath sitting behind the steering wheel.

He took the phone out and scrolled through the photographs. The last two were of Gropper. Odds were they had just been sent. Gropper put the phone in the glove compartment.

He started the car and drove away.

* * *

Hector was at the beach when the call came. He didn't say anything, just listened as the voice of the other man, his ranking superior, admonished him for screwing up what was supposed to be an easy job.

Hector knew it would be pointless to make excuses or try to dissuade the man. His only source of comfort came from the fact he'd received the phone call in the first place, and not two shots in the back of the skull. The phone meant there was a way out for him. A chance to correct his mistake. It would cost him, certainly, and there would be no more second chances after this.

He groveled a bit, as was expected of him, made the concessions they knew he'd make to appease them, then stated he'd finally take care of this problem.

Hector hung up. He pushed the camera icon and stared at the photo of the man who had caused him so much grief.

Luz dove into the pool and broke his concentration. He put the phone down and returned to the pool. He sat on the edge as she swam over.

"Everything all right?" she asked.

"Fine, just some minor work troubles."

Hector slid off the edge and into the cool water. He would make the arrangements in a moment. It might take a while for them to track down their mystery man, but Hector would put his full resources into it this time.

He'd underestimated his foe, a mistake he would not make again.

"Hi, my name is Stacy, and I'm an addict."

"Hi Stacy," the group said.

She played with the Styrofoam coffee cup in her hand. The church basement smelled of mildew and stale cigarettes even though they didn't let anyone smoke inside. She had been clean for a few days now, but every hour was still a struggle. Janice was with a relative who'd agreed to watch her. Stacy wasn't fit to be anyone's mother, but she could be a cousin. That was fine.

She still couldn't bring herself to talk about what had happened, or even say Maurice's name, but she vowed to stay clean for him.

The nightmares still caused her to wake screaming, covered in fetid sweat. It would take a few moments to realize it was a dream, then the torrents would open, and she would wail. Maurice's face would be an after image forever burned into her memory.

She did her best to go to as many meetings as she could. She met with a grief counselor. She was humble now and that was a good start.

Her sponsor had told her that in time all wounds heal, even the ones that aren't physical. If you let them. Don't linger in the past, and let the dead bury the dead. Her sponsor's bedside manner left a lot to be desired, but she spoke the truth. Stacy would make it through this, as she had so many other things in her life.

The nightmares would leave. It would just take some time.

She listened to the group go from person to person, relating their stories and what wisdom they'd picked up over time. Eventually, they joined hands, said the inspirational message they always did to close out meetings, and dispersed quietly. Outside, Stacy lit a cigarette and sat down on the steps leading to the church. It was somewhat disorienting to feel like she had nowhere to be.

"Mind if I join you?"

Stacy hadn't noticed the man until she heard him. It was a little disconcerting, his appearance out of thin air, but he didn't seem threatening.

"Not at all."

He sat down on the same step a few feet away. She took a drag and waited for him to say something, but he didn't. A minute went by, and she felt herself relaxing to in his presence. She felt safe. It was a strange feeling.

She had seen him at the meetings. He sat in the back and kept to himself.

"My father was a big scotch drinker," the man said. He stared straight ahead.

"I never liked the stuff. It was always too bitter." He continued, "My old man would laugh, and tell me eventually it turned sweet if you drank enough of it. I wonder if endurance works the same way."

The man faced her now.

"My name is Gropper."

"Stacy," she said.

"If you need anything, I'll be around."

The emotions came pretty quickly. She wasn't expecting them. She closed her eyes and nodded. When she opened her eyes, he was already gone.

McGill had just forked pecan pie into his mouth when Carmine arrived. He was escorted by a guy twice his size whose jerky movements suggested he dabbled in pharmaceuticals. He had full-sleeve tattoos and could barely fit through the door. Carmine spotted McGill, smiled, and rubbed his chest.

Carmine sat down in the booth while his muscle

lingered by the door.

"So," Carmine said.

McGill sat back and wiped his mouth.

"What? Nothing smart to say now?"

"Let me tell you how this is going to work, so you don't get your hopes up." McGill sneered.

"Oh, please," Carmine said.

"You're assuming because you brought man-mountain there, I'm going to shit my pants."

"Something like that."

"I'm guessing you paid them pretty well." McGill killed his Mickey's.

"Two for two so far. When does this get good?"

"Patience."

Carmine put his hands up. He had all the time in the world.

McGill took another bite of pecan pie. He savored this one and chewed until it was almost a paste.

"Now, to disappoint you." McGill wiped his mouth. "You ever hear the quotation, 'I am the punishment of God. If you had not committed great sins, God would not have sent a punishment like me upon you'?"

"No. The Bible?" Carmine said.

"Genghis Khan."

"You really like to talk, don't you?"

"A few years ago, Gropper came to me with a

problem. Seems he pissed off some important people, and they wanted him dead. These were people who would not be placated." McGill forked the rest of his pie into his mouth and chewed. He chased it with coffee. Carmine tried to look in control, but he was skittish around the eyes, and he drummed his fingers on the table.

"I gave him the means, and he vanished. He was gone for about a year. I told him he didn't owe me anything, but he feels obligated."

McGill took another sip of coffee.

Carmine began to look annoyed.

"And your fucking point?"

"My point?"

McGill gestured back to where Carmine's muscle had been. Gropper stood there instead. The legs of the man-mountain jutted out from behind a booth near the door.

Carmine exhaled. He licked his lips and turned back to McGill.

"Okay," he offered as if he were admiring a decent golf drive. Carmine looked from Gropper to McGill.

"You can come back with all the help you want. Pay them however much you want." McGill pointed toward Gropper. "Just remember, I have the punishment of God."

Carmine's hand went to reach inside his jacket, probably where he kept a piece, but he hesitated. His body sagged; a gesture which suggested he knew he had lost this one. He slid out of the booth. McGill watched him help lift his friend from the booth. The man's size made it awkward. Gropper took the now-vacant seat across from McGill. The waiter brought over coffee for Gropper and another Mickey's.

Things had been quiet since the dust settled at the motel. Gropper flexed his hand once and took a sip of his coffee. The slaughter had been in the papers for two days, then the interest died down. It was still an open case, but the Cuban had been a pro, so Gropper was certain all leads would dead end. He kept tabs on the cousin, and she wasn't going to look into anything, content to move on with her life. She wouldn't be a loose end.

"Have you heard back?" Gropper said.

"I have." McGill took the piece of paper from his pocket and slid it across the table.

"Guy's name is Hector Rodriguez."

Gropper opened the paper, memorized the information, and slid it back to McGill.

"You sure you want to do this?" McGill asked.

Gropper didn't say anything.

"Just thought I'd ask," McGill said.

"If things go south…" Gropper said.

"I'll take care of it."

Gropper had arranged for McGill to spread his assets among John and Ms. Bradley. He would also wipe his identity clean to avoid any blowback.

"I should be back in a few days," Gropper said. McGill sneered.

"Have a piece of pie before you go."

Gropper paused for a second and then said, "Sure."

McGill signaled the waiter and McGill ordered another two slices of pecan pie.

The two men ate in silence.

Gropper sat on the stool watching the dance floor in the reflection of the mirror above the bar. The place was packed. South Beach on a Saturday night. The neon and strobe kept the shadows dancing on the floor, and the smell of the fog machine permeated the air. He stayed focused on the VIP enclave on the second floor and watched Hector pouring drinks.

Off to the sides stood some large men in suits. Probably a mix of those who worked at the club, as well as Hector's personal guard.

"Another?" the bartender asked. One of three working, they made sure to keep the customers occupied. She was a bronzed blonde with zero fat on her body.

"Yeah," Gropper said.

She went away and returned with his whiskey. He drank it back, then shut his eyes and blocked out the sound of the music, the conversations, everything happening around him, until time slowed to a crawl.

At some point, Hector would leave to use the bathroom.

One bodyguard would go with him, the others would remain by the velvet rope. Gropper decided to head to the bathroom and take out the bodyguard. Hector would probably have a piece, but he was not a killer. He was soft, used to having other people do the dirty work, and it would be his undoing. Gropper would make it fast and effective. He rolled the newspaper in his hands. They might still come for him and McGill, but this would slow them down.

Gropper ordered one more drink.

He watched Hector rise and head for the bathroom. Gropper stood up and gripped the Millwall brick in his hand.

He reached into his pocket and pressed the button on the device. He'd rigged a smoke bomb near the entrance. It would only take a minute to set off the sprinklers and fire alarm. The staff would be forced to evacuate the patrons.

Gropper hugged the edge of the dance floor, keeping close to the bar. He navigated through people until he made his way toward the stairs. Eyeing Hector as he and his subordinate disappeared around the corner, Gropper climbed the stairs toward the bathroom.

Around the corner, the carpeting muffled some of the sound from the dance floor, but it was still loud enough. The bodyguard stood outside of the bathroom door. He was instantly alert to Gropper's presence. The man saw the brick, sensed something amiss, and went for his own weapon. The element of surprise gone, Gropper charged. The bodyguard was fast but underestimated Gropper's speed. His expandable baton snapped open, but Gropper hit the man's wrist with the brick, and it flew to the ground. The bodyguard unloaded a punch and kick combination which he probably worked time and time again in the gym.

But this wasn't the gym.

Gropper blocked the man's left hook, then hit the man with the brick. The guy staggered back, and Gropper hit him twice more. The guy careened into the wall and passed out on the floor. The brick had begun to lose some of its effectiveness, so Gropper traded it for the baton.

Pushing the bathroom door open, Gropper spotted Hector at the sink, checking himself in the mirror. He did a double take when he saw Gropper.

"*Chinga*," Hector said.

His tone was one more of awe than fear.

Hector reached for his piece. Gropper threw the baton. Hector blocked it with his forearm, but Gropper was already on him.

Gropper assumed a wrist lock on the gun hand and flipped Hector onto the ground. Hector wheezed as the air was knocked out of him. Gropper snapped the wrist, took the piece, removed the clip. Hector's scream reverberated around the walls. Gropper threw the gun into one of the toilets and the clip into another. Hector had gotten to his knees and was holding his wrist.

He was tougher than Gropper originally pegged him for.

"You can't kill me," Hector said through gritted teeth.

"No?"

"It'd be suicide."

Gropper stood in front of him.

"I've had worse trouble."

The fire alarm went off. Hector made a move for the door. Gropper was already in front of him. The bravado now gone, Hector tried to escape farther into the bathroom. He made it to the wall, near the urinals, and yelled.

Gropper punched him twice, then smashed his head into the porcelain rim of the urinal. The vibrations passed through Hector's body as it shook, then went flaccid. Gropper landed a shot to the base of the skull and checked for a pulse. He couldn't fine one. Gropper walked to the entrance and opened the door. The barrel of a gun emerged through the entrance as another bodyguard tried to gain tactical advantage. Gropper put his shoulder into it, and knocked the man backward. The weapon fired twice and bullets pinged off the tiles. Gropper made it out of the bathroom as the bodyguard tried to reset the weapon.

Gropper hit the man and swept his legs out. The man fell with a thud and was stunned.

Gropper moved quickly, past the still unconscious first bodyguard. The crowd had swelled and funneled through the exits. Gropper was sped down the stairs, merging effortlessly with the crowd, and walked out into the humid air.

His car was where he had parked it, a few blocks

away.

He steadied his breathing and waited for his heart to slow. He turned the key in the ignition, and the motor came alive. Gropper eased out into the street toward the highway.

If he made good time, he might make it back before sunrise.

ACKNOWLEDGMENTS

Thank you to Ellen, Ralph, and Adam, for reading the first few drafts. Thank you to Noa for the copyedits.

ANDREW DAVIE received an MFA from Adelphi University. He taught English in Macau on a Fulbright Grant, and he's taught English and writing in New York, Virginia, and Hong Kong. In June of 2018, he survived a ruptured aneurysm and subarachnoid hemorrhage.

asdavie.wordpress.com

On the following pages are a few
more great titles from the
Down & Out Books publishing family.

For a complete list of books and to
sign up for our newsletter,
go to DownAndOutBooks.com.

The Unknowing
Trey R. Barker

Down & Out Books
September 2019
978-1-64396-033-3

Runaway. Victim of domestic battery. An older, married boyfriend. Pregnant. And ultimately, dead and forgotten in a cornfield. For Sheriff's Deputy Wes Spahn, this case has too many similarities to his first case as a detective, similarities that will leave him questioning everything.

He tries to work both cases simultaneously and soon understands someone is gunning for him.

Which case is drawing this attention? Who wants him dead?

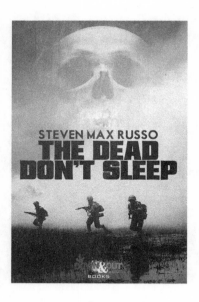

The Dead Don't Sleep
Steven Max Russo

Down & Out Books
November 2019
978-1-64396-051-7

Frank Thompson, a recent widower and aging Vietnam veteran, is down from Maine visiting his nephew in New Jersey. While at a trap range, they have a chance encounter with a strange man who claims to remember Frank from the Vietnam war.

Frank was part of a psychopathic squad of killers put together by the CIA and trained by Special Forces to cause death and mayhem during the war. That chance encounter has put three man on the squad on a collision course with the man who trained them to kill, in a nostalgic blood lust to hunt down and eliminate the professional soldier who led them long ago.

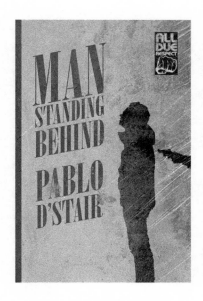

Man Standing Behind
Pablo D'Stair

All Due Respect, an imprint of
Down & Out Books
978-1-64396-035-7

Leaving work on a nondescript evening, Roger is held up at gunpoint when he stops at a cash machine. But robbery isn't on the gunman's mind...Roger is told simply to walk.

The gunman takes him on a macabre odyssey—from city pubs to suburban neighborhoods to isolated homes in the country—and as the night presses on, a seemingly not-so-random body count grows around him.

A man caught in the roils of a mortal circumstance having nothing to do with his own life. Is he a witness, a victim...or something altogether worse?

Main Bad Guy
A Love & Bullets Hookup
Nick Kolakowski

Shotgun Honey, an imprint of
Down & Out Books
978-1-948235-70-9

Bill and Fiona, the lovable anti-heroes of the "Love & Bullets" trilogy, find themselves in the toughest of tough spots: badly wounded, hunted by cops and goons, and desperately in need of a drink (or five).

After a round-the-world tour of spectacular criminality, they're back in New York. Locked in a panic room on the top floor of a skyscraper, surrounded by pretty much everyone in three zip codes who wants to kill them, they'll need to figure out how to stay upright and breathing...and maybe deal out a little payback in the process.

CPSIA information can be obtained
at www.ICGtesting.com
Printed in the USA
BVHW031623220719
554055BV00016B/2039/P

US TAX REFORM
FOR HIPSTERS

TIMUR KNYAZEV, CPA

Dedicated to my beautiful wife, **Olesya**
& my three precious kids:
Arseny, Matvey & Anisia

CONTENTS

1 / INTRODUCTION

On Friday, December 22, 2017, before leaving for his Christmas vacation at Mar-o-Lago in Florida, President Trump signed into law Public Law 115-97, also known as H.R.1, the Tax Cuts & Jobs Act of 2017 (the Act), abbreviated as TCJA & often referred to as the Trump tax cuts, the GOP tax plan, or just tax reform.

This law represents the biggest reform of the American tax system in over 30 years, since 1986, to be exact & brings dramatic changes to the already fascinating world of US tax.

The Act itself, one of the stated goals of which was tax simplification, is over 1,000 pages long & it contains some of the most complex & confusing tax rules ever written. How is that for simplification?

Book structure

In this book, I will try to summarize the key provisions of the tax reform law & discuss how these will affect individuals & businesses of different types. The focus of this book is on US federal taxation. Just to be clear – tax reform changed our federal tax law & did not directly amend any state laws, although many states do follow federal tax provisions via a concept known as conformity with the Internal Revenue Code.

Throughout the book, I may refer to the changes introduced as part of tax reform as the 'new law' or 'new rules' to differentiate from the 'old law' or 'old rules,' which I will also bring up for comparison & reference purposes.

There's no way for us to cover all the changes, so we will concentrate on the major tax provisions.

Here & there you will also notice links to relevant tax code sections in the following format:

 IRC Section #

Since many of you might be new to tax concepts altogether, before I dive into the tax reform changes in each area, I will try to do a quick introduction & provide a general overview of the topic in question.

A couple of important notes & recommendations about this book:

Research & analyze beyond this book

This book is designed to provide a general high-level overview of the US tax reform legislation enacted in December 2017. Tax law is complicated stuff with lots of tricky exceptions & special rules, so if you are trying to research & analyze a particular matter in-depth, please make sure to do so using reliable sources, such as the tax code itself (formally known as the Internal Revenue Code), reputable research resources, the IRS website (irs.gov) & publications by the Big 4 accounting firms (in case you don't know the Big 4, they are: EY, PwC, KPMG & Deloitte) or other trusted sources. This book should be a good starting point for your quest, as it will give you some relevant keywords & references to tax code sections to start your search for more detailed insight & guidance.

Hire a professional

This book is not a substitute for professional tax advice. In fact, I urge you not to act on anything you read in this book, without consulting a qualified tax pro. I'm sure this book will help you learn more about taxes & possibly answer some general questions, but please remember that nothing replaces professional advice by a qualified tax accountant or attorney. This book is intended for general educational purposes only & does not take into account the specific facts & circumstances of any given tax situation or transaction, each of which is generally unique. Even when you think your situation is super easy & you can do it all yourself, I still strongly recommend to consult with a qualified tax specialist, such as a state licensed CPA (Certified Public Accountant), an IRS EA (Enrolled Agent) or a tax attorney admitted to practice in your state. Would you represent yourself in court without a lawyer, or try to treat a medical condition without a doctor? Probably not. Then why take a risk in a sensitive space like taxes? Tax is not a do-it-yourself kind of area. Hire a professional.

By the way, this is my first book, so once you are done reading it, please make sure to leave a review on Amazon! Thanks for your support!

Timur

Timur Knyazev, CPA

P.S. check out my website @ **timurk.com**

& follow me on Instagram @ **timur.cpa**

2 / PERSONAL TAX

Are you excited yet? Let's get this book started for real & kick it off with personal tax matters. After all, that's what it all comes down to, or as Mitt Romney put it: "Corporations are people, my friend, everything corporations earn ultimately goes to people. Where do you think it goes?"

So, when talking about US personal (aka individual) taxes – the starting point is to determine who is subject to them. All **US citizens & green card holders** are automatically treated as tax residents of the United States, no matter where they live or work. That is our **citizenship taxation** regime at work & tax reform didn't change that aspect of our personal tax system.

Now, as always in the world of tax, there could be some exceptions from this rule. For instance, certain green card holders teamed up with great tax advisors might find a way to build a well-supported tax case & justify that even though they possess a green card, they remained tax residents of another country & should be treated as non-residents for US tax purposes, but that kind of position is a rare exception, it has its risks & can only be established based on an in-depth & very comprehensive analysis of all facts & circumstances pertaining to the individual, their family, their earnings, assets & activities.

Ok, what if you are not a lucky American citizen or green card holder, then what? Then you count your days to determine if you are a resident of this country. You have to figure out if you met the so-called **'substantial presence test'**, a tricky calculation of your days spent in the US that involves looking at the current tax year, as well as prior years, but if you want an oversimplified version – it's in line with the typical residency tests around the world – if you spent over 6 months (183 days) in the US in a given tax year, you are generally a tax resident for that year. During your first or last years in the US (let's say you are here on a work assignment for a few years) things can get interesting & you might be a 'dual status resident', which means a non-resident for part of the year & a resident for the other part of the same year, i.e., residency starting on the day you entered the country / ending on the day you left.

If you are a **US citizen or resident alien, your worldwide income is subject to US income tax**, regardless of where you reside or where the income originated.

What if you are not even in the US that much & again, you have no US citizenship & no green card? Well, then you are a **non-resident** of the United States. What this means is that you will be subject to tax in the US **only if you have US source income.**

Let me give you a couple of good examples of US source income – let's say you are a foreign national & you live in your home country, but you happen to own & rent out an apartment in Downtown Brooklyn, or DoBro for short (in this example you are receiving income from a US situated property); or maybe you are a famous European DJ that came to the US to play a deep house set at Ultra Music Festival in Miami (in this instance you are a foreign resident performing personal services on US soil). In situations like these, you will most likely trigger a requirement to file a non-resident tax return (IRS form 1040NR) to report your US income on the federal level & may need a state level filing too.

Additionally, parties making payments to you as a non-resident for services performed in the US (e.g., Ultra sending you the payment in the DJ example above) will most likely have a withholding tax requirement, i.e., they will need to keep 30% of your pay & send it to the IRS. Passive types of income, such as royalties, interest, dividends originating in the US are generally subject to US withholding taxes too.

In order to better understand the impact of the new law, you will need to know how US personal taxes are calculated on a typical individual tax return (IRS form 1040):

A. We start by capturing all types of income, including wages, tips, self-employment, partnership income, capital gains, interest, dividends, rents, royalties, etc. Not sure if something constitutes income? Most likely it does, as virtually everything you earn or receive is considered part of gross income, with rare exceptions.

 IRC Section 61

B. Next, we get to take some deductions & make some adjustments directly against gross income, which are called 'above-the-line' deductions. Examples of such deductions include the foreign earned income exclusion (under IRC Section 911), retirement account contributions, moving & education expenses, alimony payments & the deductible portion of self-employment tax, to name a few.

C. Then, we take gross income (**A**) adjusted by the 'above-the-line' deductions (**B**) which brings us to a magic line called **'adjusted gross income' or AGI.** This is an important number on the return as it is often used to determine whether or not you qualify for certain deductions or exemptions & how much of these you can claim.

D. Now that you have your **AGI** locked in, you get to the part where you deduct from AGI your **standard deduction OR your itemized deductions** (not both).

Prior to tax reform, you would then also take your personal exemptions (one for each member of your family or household), but as you will soon learn, personal exemptions have been temporarily suspended by the new law.

E. Now that you have reduced your AGI by your standard deduction or itemized deductions, you arrive at **taxable income**. That's another important number, which will help determine how much tax will be due & may be used to figure out if you are eligible for certain credits & tax benefits.

F. Now that you know your **taxable income**, your **regular income tax** is calculated on that taxable income, using the tax rate applicable to your filing status & income bracket, as presented on IRS tax tables, which you can find in the IRS form 1040 instructions.

G. You think you are done now? Not just yet. In addition to the regular tax, you may be subject to the **alternative minimum tax (AMT)** & a few other special taxes, which may increase your total tax liability.

But this final section of the return is not just about bad news (like taxes you owe!), it's also about credits, or, said differently, reductions to your tax liability. That's where you get to take your child tax credit, foreign tax credit (FTC), earned income tax credit (EITC) & other credits.

Any taxes that your employer withheld from your salary (shown on box 2 on your form w-2) or that you paid yourself by making estimated tax payments will also be reflected in this last section of the return & will be used to determine if you owe any additional taxes, or if the IRS owes you a refund.

As they say, a picture is worth a thousand words & a good table is probably worth even more, so let's put all this in a table summarizing all the steps in the calculation, so you can clearly visualize the general structure of a personal US tax return & where all the pieces of the puzzle fit:

all sources of taxable income

= gross income

- above-the-line deductions

= adjusted gross income (AGI)

- standard or itemized deductions

= taxable income

+/- other taxes, credits, taxes paid or withheld

= balance due or refund

The **difference between tax credits & tax deductions** is that deductions reduce your taxable income, while credits reduce your ultimate tax liability. So typically credits give you bigger cash tax savings compared to deductions. Let's say you are in the 10% tax bracket. A $1,000 deduction will result in a reduction to taxable income in that amount & therefore a reduction of your tax bill by 100 dollars ($1,000 x 10%), while a $1,000 credit will save you $1,000 in actual taxes. A dramatic ten times difference. The moral of the story - don't confuse deductions & credits.

Ok, now let's get to tax reform!

It's important to note right away that almost all of the individual tax reform changes, including the new gift & estate tax rules, which will be discussed in the following chapter, are all **temporary** & are **set to expire** (we tax people say the rules will 'sunset') in just eight years. So enjoy these tax cuts while they last. The new rates & provisions will apply to **tax years 2018 through 2025 only** unless extended by future legislation.

You will note that I don't use the words 'repealed' or 'eliminated' with respect to any deductions or tax benefits that have been temporarily affected by the law, but rather use the term 'suspended' which is a more appropriate word to use given the temporary nature of the personal tax provisions in the Act.

Dec 31  **2025**

When the Times Square ball drops marking the beginning of 2026, the rules will magically **revert to their pre-2018 form**, i.e., back to the old rules that were in effect for 2017 & many previous tax years. Future legislation will be required to make any of the temporary provisions discussed below effective beyond 2025.

A few individual items in the bill are permanent, however.

PERMANENT CHANGES

- The indirect effective **repeal of the Obamacare 'individual mandate'**, which was achieved by reducing the individual responsibility payment down to zero, so no need to worry about the penalty for not having health insurance... starting with tax year 2019 & hopefully never again!

The individual mandate clause of the Affordable Care Act (aka Obamacare) requires individuals to buy insurance or pay a penalty at tax time unless they qualify for an exemption. Republicans didn't succeed in repealing & replacing Obamacare, but they changed that penalty, which was in the tax code, to zero.

 IRC Section 5000A

- Introduction of a new **slower inflation indexing method** for tax rate brackets, standard deduction amounts & other thresholds. Under old law, annual inflation adjustments were made by reference to the consumer price index (CPI). The new law uses the 'chained CPI' method, which takes into account consumers' preference for cheaper substitute goods during periods of inflation. Chained CPI is expected to result in smaller annual increases to indexed amounts.

 IRC Section 1(f)(3)

- **Alimony changes** - in divorce situations, one spouse or ex-spouse may become legally obligated to make payments to the other. Because these payments are often substantial, locking in tax deductions for the payer has often been an important issue. Before the enactment of the TCJA, payments that met the definition of alimony could always be deducted by the payer for federal income tax purposes & recipients of alimony payments had to report the payments as taxable income. The Act changed the tax treatment of alimony.

 IRC Sections 61(a)(8), 71, 215

For divorces & legal separations that are executed in 2019 & later, the alimony-paying spouse won't be able to deduct the payments, while the alimony-receiving spouse will no longer include payments in gross income.

TCJA rules don't apply to pre-2019 divorce & separation agreements, so old law treatment continues to apply unless parties agree otherwise & the court approves the arrangement. If allowed, alimony is deducted 'above-the-line.'

Now, again, the rest of the personal stuff discussed below is all **temporary & good for tax years 2018 through 2025 only**.

FILING STATUSES

The new law retains the same good old five filing statuses below that we're all so used to & love so much:

1. **Single**
2. **Married filing joint (MFJ)**
3. **Married filing separate (MFS)**
4. **Head of household (HOH)**
5. **Qualifying widow/widower with dependent child**

The first two are by far the most popular. All these statuses are pretty self-explanatory, except the often misunderstood 'head of household' status, so let's talk about that one in a little more detail.

Head of household ('HOH') is a filing status for single or unmarried taxpayers who keep up a home for qualifying people (generally, your dependents, which could be your kids, parents or certain relatives you support). HOH has some important tax advantages over the Single filing status. If you qualify as HOH, you will have a lower tax rate & a higher standard deduction than a Single filer.

Here's what it takes to qualify for this status:

- You were single, divorced, legally separated, or were 'considered unmarried' on the last day of the tax year

- You paid more than half the cost of 'keeping up a home' for the year
- A 'qualifying person' lived with you in that home for more than half the year, except for temporary absences (a dependent parent is not required to live with you)

TAX RATES

 IRC Section 1

The personal income tax rate structure changed: it stayed progressive, with seven brackets, but with **lower rates & higher income thresholds**. The best way to illustrate these changes is using the side by side comparable rate tables for the two most popular filing statuses:

Single

2018 – Prior Law		2018 – New Law	
Tax Rate	If taxable income is:	Tax Rate	If taxable income is:
10%	$0 to $9,525	10%	$0 to $9,525
15%	$9,526 to $38,700	12%	$9,526 to $38,700
25%	$38,701 to $93,700	22%	$38,701 to $82,500
28%	$93,701 to $195,450	24%	$82,501 to $157,500
33%	$195,451 to $424,950	32%	$157,501 to $200,000
35%	$424,951 to $426,700	35%	$200,001 to $500,000
39.6%	$426,701 or more	37%	$500,001 or more

Married filing joint

2018 – Prior Law		2018 – New Law	
Tax Rate	If taxable income is:	Tax Rate	If taxable income is:
10%	$0 to $19,050	10%	$0 to $19,050
15%	$19,051 to $77,400	12%	$19,051 to $77,400
25%	$77,401 to $156,150	22%	$77,401 to $165,000
28%	$156,151 to $237,950	24%	$165,001 to $315,000
33%	$237,951 to $424,950	32%	$315,001 to $400,000
35%	$424,951 to $480,050	35%	$400,001 to $600,000
39.6%	$480,051 or more	37%	$600,001 or more

INDIVIDUAL AMT

 IRC Section 55(d)(4)

Unfortunately, the Act did not repeal the individual **alternative minimum tax (AMT)** altogether, but temporarily increased both the exemption amounts & the phase-out threshold for individuals:

- For joint filers, the AMT exemption amount for 2018 increased from $84.5k under the old law to $109.4k. The phase-out threshold went up from $160.9k to $1 million
- The exemption increased from $54.3k to $70.3k for most other individual taxpayers, while their phase-out level increased from $120.7k to $500k

This means that if your income is below the new higher exemption amount you are fully exempt from this tax & if your income is below the phase-out amount you are likely partially exempt & even if you are a high-income taxpayer it doesn't automatically mean AMT will be due, the answer depends on a bunch of factors. In practice, the combination of increased exemptions & limits on AMT preference items like the state & local deduction should reduce the number of taxpayers subject to AMT under the new law, at least over the next eight years when these rules are in effect.

STANDARD DEDUCTIONS

 IRC Section 63(c)(7)

Good news! The new law significantly increased (almost doubled!) the **standard deductions**. The amounts for tax year 2018 are as follows (these amounts will be indexed / adjusted for inflation in future years using the new slower chained CPI method we discussed earlier):

- Single or married filing separate - **$12k in 2018** (up from $6.35k in 2017)
- Married filing joint or surviving spouses - **$24k in 2018** (up from $12.7k in 2017)
- Head of household - **$18k in 2018** (up from $9.35k in 2017)

What this effectively means is that a single taxpayer making $12k or a married couple making $24k in wages will not pay any federal income tax. In fact, it's likely that people making less than these thresholds in wages will not even have a filing requirement. For self-employment income, the threshold requiring tax filings is generally much lower.

The new law retains the add-ons to the standard deductions for the aged, the blind & the disabled, which are $1.3k for married taxpayers & $1.6k for unmarried taxpayers.

PERSONAL EXEMPTIONS

Now, some not so good news. The **personal exemptions** (both personal & dependent ones) are getting **suspended** for tax years 2018 through 2025. For tax year 2017 personal exemptions were set at $4,050 & one was allowed for every person in your family / household. A pretty good tax benefit, especially for big families.

But don't start crying just yet if you have a lot of kids & loved these exemptions, Congress enhanced & expanded the child tax credit, which we will discuss soon below. For most taxpayers with kids, it should provide an even higher tax benefit than the now suspended personal exemptions used to give.

ABOVE-THE-LINE DEDUCTIONS

MOVING EXPENSES

The moving expenses deduction used to be a great perk for people who relocated – an 'above-the-line' deduction, meaning that it directly reduced adjusted gross income (AGI). It has now been **suspended**.

Additionally, any relocation allowances or move-related reimbursements from employers are now taxable to the employee. As a result of these changes, job relocations will certainly become a more costly exercise.

This deduction remains available for members of the Armed Forces.

WHISTLEBLOWER PROGRAM

The Act provides a new above-the-line deduction for attorney & court expenses paid by whistleblowers.

QUALIFIED TUITION

The Act retains the deduction for qualified tuition, student loan interest & related expenses.

ITEMIZED DEDUCTIONS

With the higher standard deductions discussed above, many taxpayers will likely not need to itemize deductions on Schedule A anymore. On top of the by-now-famous 'doubling of the standard deduction,' there are some new changes & limitations to itemized deductions, many of which also seem to be designed to discourage taxpayers from itemizing deductions.

Let's go through these:

STATE & LOCAL TAXES (AKA 'SALT')

The most talked about change. Under the new law, itemized deductions for state & local income taxes, property taxes & sales/use taxes are **limited to $10k per year** in the aggregate (not indexed for inflation!). The limitation does not apply if the taxes are incurred in carrying on a trade or business or otherwise incurred for the production of income (e.g., property taxes for an apartment that you are renting out).

There was no limitation specific to the state & local deduction in the old law.

In addition, foreign real property taxes, other than those incurred in a trade or business, are no longer eligible for the deduction.

MORTGAGE INTEREST

The new law limits the deduction available for **mortgage interest** by reducing the amount of debt that is treated as qualified acquisition indebtedness from the currently allowed level of $1 million down to $750k. Debt incurred before December 15, 2017, is not affected by the reduction & is, therefore 'grandfathered.' When something is 'grandfathered' it means it's exempt from a new law or regulation.

Additionally, any debt incurred before December 15, 2017, but refinanced later, continues to be covered by old law & the higher $1 million limitation, to the extent the debt resulting from the refinancing does not exceed the balance of the debt immediately prior to refinancing.

The deduction for interest paid on a home equity line of credit (HELOC) or similar home equity driven debt has been suspended.

CHARITABLE DONATIONS

This deduction is not going anywhere. The new law increases the adjusted gross income (AGI) limitation for **charitable contributions** of cash made by individuals to public charities & certain private foundations to 60% of AGI (from the old 50% limitation). There have been some reports in the media suggesting that the deductibility of charitable donations may be adversely affected by the tax reform bill – this isn't the case, as the new law retains this itemized deduction & even increases the AGI percentage limitation.

Non-cash charitable donations continue to be deductible & the mileage deduction relating to miles driven in service of charitable organizations remained unchanged at 14 cents for tax year 2018.

PERSONAL CASUALTY LOSSES

Under old law, a deduction could be claimed for any loss sustained during the tax year that is not compensated by insurance or otherwise, subject to certain limitations. The new law temporarily limits the deduction for personal casualty & theft losses to losses incurred **only in federally-declared disaster areas**.

MEDICAL EXPENSES

You are allowed to deduct qualified out of pocket medical expenses that exceed 7.5% of your adjusted gross income (AGI) for 2018 (no change from the pre-reform law). Beginning on January 1, 2019, however, you can deduct only the amount of the total unreimbursed allowable medical care expenses for the year that exceeds 10% of your AGI. In practice, this means your medical expenses need to be pretty high relative to your income to 'activate' this itemized deduction.

For instance, if your AGI is $50k in 2019 & you incurred $6k in qualified medical expenses, you would multiply $50k by 0.1 (10%) to determine that only expenses exceeding $5k can be deducted. This leaves you with a deduction of $1k ($6k - $5k).

The IRS allows you to deduct preventative care, treatments, surgeries, dental & vision care as qualifying medical expenses. You can also deduct visits to psychologists & psychiatrists. Prescription medication, medical devices & products such as glasses, contacts, hearing aids are also deductible. You can also deduct travel expenses related to medical care such as mileage on your car, bus fare & parking fees.

Any medical expenses for which you are reimbursed by an insurance company or otherwise cannot be deducted. Plus, deductions for cosmetic procedures are generally disallowed, as well as the cost of non-prescription or other purchases for general health such as toothpaste, vitamins, etc.

WAGERING / GAMBLING LOSSES

Under the new law, those who itemize deductions will continue to be able to deduct gambling losses up to the amount of their total winnings.

The new law **will impact those who meet the IRS's narrow definition of a 'professional gambler' or 'wager'** by providing that any expenses incurred in connection with the gambling activity (e.g., hotel stays, transportation, etc.) should also be captured as losses allowable only to the extent of winnings. As an example, a professional gambler who has $100k in winnings can deduct up to that amount in combined losses & expenses such as travel, meals & hotel stays. Prior to these recent changes, professional gamblers were allowed to separately deduct expenses incurred in carrying out wagering transactions.

OTHER DEDUCTIONS & OVERALL LIMITATION

Under old law, individuals were able to claim itemized deductions for certain miscellaneous expenses, for example, investment fees & charges, unreimbursed business expenses, tax preparation fees & safe deposit box rental fees. These items were not deductible unless, in aggregate, the expenses exceeded 2% of the taxpayer's adjusted gross income (AGI), a requirement referred to as the '2% floor'. The new law **suspends all miscellaneous itemized deductions** that were subject to the '2% floor'.

Under old law, the total amount of allowable itemized deductions (with the exception of medical expenses, investment interest expenses, casualty, theft or gambling losses) was reduced by 3% of the amount by which the taxpayer's AGI exceeded a threshold amount (referred to as the 'Pease' limitation, named after Congressman Donald Pease who originally introduced the legislation in 1991). The new law **suspends the overall 'Pease' limitation** on itemized deductions. A positive development for taxpayers that will still continue to itemize.

CAPITAL GAINS

No changes to our capital gains system of taxation: long-term capital gains are still defined as gains made on assets that you held for over a year, while short-term capital gains are from assets you held for a year or less. Long-term gains are taxed at reduced rates of 0%, 15%, or 20%, depending on your tax bracket, while short-term gains are taxed as ordinary income at the new rates discussed above.

The new law doesn't align the long-term capital gain rate brackets with the ordinary income ones, so long-term capital gains will be taxed as follows:

Long-Term Capital Gains Rate	Single Taxpayers	Married Filing Jointly
0%	Up to $38,600	Up to $77,200
15%	$38,600-$425,800	$77,200-479,000
20%	Over $425,800	Over $479,000

These reduced rates also continue to apply to **qualified dividends**.

ADDITIONAL MEDICARE TAX & NET INVESTMENT INCOME TAX (NIIT)

The two Obamacare surcharge taxes have not been eliminated & still apply to taxpayers with certain types of income in excess of:

- $250k for married filing joint couples
- $125k for married filing separate taxpayers
- $200k for single & HOH filers

The **0.9% Additional Medicare Tax** applies to the amount of wages & self-employment income that exceeds the threshold amounts above, bringing the total marginal tax rate for some earned income to

37.9% (37% regular tax rate + 0.9% additional Medicare tax).

The Net Investment Income Tax or NIIT applies at a rate of 3.8% to certain net investment income of individuals, estates & trusts that have adjusted gross income (AGI) in excess of the threshold amounts presented above. In general, investment income includes, but is not limited to interest, dividends, capital gains, rent & royalty income, certain annuities, income from businesses involved in trading of financial instruments or commodities & business income that is deemed passive to the taxpayer. The NIIT may result in the total marginal tax rate for certain unearned income to be as high as 40.8% (37% regular tax rate + 3.8% NIIT).

KIDDIE TAX

Once upon a time, a popular tax strategy for high-income families was to assign passive investments & unearned income (such as dividends, interest & capital gains) to their kids, to reduce their overall family tax bill, i.e., the assumption here is that the kids are in lower tax brackets & would, therefore, enjoy lower tax rates.

In the 1980's the 'kiddie tax' was adopted to combat this practice by taxing certain amounts of children's unearned income at the parents' tax rate instead of the child's typically lower rate. That rate could be as high as 39.6%, compared to the 10% rate that most children would be paying.

Starting in 2018 & scheduled to continue through 2025, **the TCJA changes the 'kiddie tax' rates**. During these years, children's unearned income will not be taxed at their parents' income tax rates like before. Instead, all net unearned income over a threshold amount ($2,100 for 2018) gets taxed using the brackets & rates for trusts & estates.

For 2018 these rates are as follows:

- **Up to $2,550**   10%
- **$2,550 to $9,150**   24%
- **$9,150 to $12,500**   35%
- **Over $12,500**   37%

The change simplifies the 'kiddie tax' by applying a single set of rates to children's unearned income. Plus, a child's tax rate is no longer affected by his or her parents' tax situation or the unearned income of siblings. Depending on the specifics of the situation the child's income may need to be reported on a separate tax return filed by the child or included on the parent's return.

Kids' earned income, such as wages from a summer job, is taxed at rates applicable to single filers.

CHILD TAX CREDIT

The new law increases the child tax credit to $2k per qualifying child (from the old $1k). The law also temporarily provides a $500 nonrefundable credit for qualifying dependents other than qualifying children.

Thanks to Marco Rubio, who threatened to withhold his vote over it, $1.4k of this child tax credit is now **refundable**, which means that you may be able to get a refund in excess of the tax withheld from your pay, i.e., a refundable credit can get you a cash tax refund even if you have no tax liability. The AGI levels at which this credit starts to phase-out increased from $110k under old law to $400k for joint filers & from $75k to $200k for single filers.

In the tax language, 'phase-out' refers to a credit or benefit going away, generally, because certain income levels are achieved. In other words, a situation when a tax credit or another tax benefit starts gradually disappearing because your income exceeds certain thresholds. When your income is above the maximum level in the phase-out range, you no longer qualify for the benefit in question at all.

Additionally, the earned income threshold for the refundable child tax credit was lowered from $3k under old law to $2.5k, meaning it's enough for you to earn just $2.5k in wages or from self-employment for the year to start enjoying this credit.

RETIREMENT SAVINGS

The Act generally retains the current rules for IRA, 401(k) & other retirement plans, but eliminates the ability to reverse a Roth IRA conversion back to a traditional IRA.

Additionally, TCJA extends the amount of time taxpayers have to repay a loan taken from their retirement account from 60 days to the due date of the return (including extensions).

RETAINED PROVISIONS

EARNED INCOME TAX CREDIT (EITC)

Many of you may be familiar with the EITC (Earned Income Tax Credit), which is one of America's most effective anti-poverty tools in the tax code, helping millions of low-income American workers with a few thousand dollars when they file their taxes.

No worries if you are an EITC recipient. The new tax law **doesn't make any changes to the EITC rules**. The only item that may indirectly affect it is the slower 'Chained CPI' inflation indexing discussed in the Permanent Changes section above.

EXPAT / NOMAD DEDUCTIONS & CREDITS

It's important to mention that the tax breaks available to US expats & digital nomads **remained**

in place, including the foreign earned income exclusion taken on IRS form 2555 & the foreign tax credit on IRS form 1116. Tax treaty positions on IRS form 8833 also remain available for any taxpayers that need to tackle double tax situations arising from their cross-border activities or transactions.

OTHER KEY PROVISIONS REMAINING INTACT

- Gain from sale of your primary residence continues to be fully excludable from taxation up to certain limits – that's a big one that people were worried about!
- Tax credit for qualified adoption expenses & exclusion of any such expenses paid or reimbursed by your employer
- 15% disability credit, available to every citizen & resident over 65 or retired on permanent & total disability
- Mortgage credit certificate (MCC) program
- Qualified plug-in electric vehicle credit under IRC Section 30D
- American opportunity tax credit (AOTC)
- Deduction for contributions to an Archer medical savings account (MSA) & exclusion of employer contributions
- $5k annual exclusion for employer-provided dependent care assistance
- Exclusion of interest on US savings bonds used to pay for higher education

3 / WEALTH TRANSFERS

Estate & gift taxes are imposed on the federal level on the transfer of property from one person to another, either at death (**estate tax**) or while the giver of the property is still alive (**gift tax**).

Additionally, there's a special **generation-skipping transfer tax (GSTT)** imposed on both gifts & transfers to (or for the benefit of) unrelated persons who are more than 37.5 years younger than the donor or to related persons more than one generation younger than the donor, such as grandchildren. The GSTT was created in response to strategies involving wealth transfers to grandkids & other decedents in order to avoid paying estate taxes generation after generation.

Estates are required to file a federal estate tax return (IRS form 706) if the value of the **gross estate**, minus certain deductions, is above a **personal exemption** amount discussed below. The gross estate includes the value of all property in which the decedent had an interest at the time of his or her death - including such items as real estate, stocks & bonds, other investments & cash, insurance on the decedent's life & jointly owned property. If spouses own property jointly & one dies, one half of the value of the property is included in the gross estate of the deceased spouse. Any debts of the decedent (such as mortgages) are deducted in calculating the gross estate.

A deceased person's estate **can pass tax-free to a surviving spouse**, as long as the surviving spouse is a US citizen & the deceased spouse's interest in the estate passes directly to the surviving spouse. This rule is called the **unlimited marital deduction**.

Deductions against the gross estate include certain administrative expenses, funeral expenses, claims against the estate, certain taxes, other indebtedness & charitable bequests.

Gift tax is a tax on the transfer of property from one person to another, during the giving person's lifetime. Certain gifts are exempt from the gift tax, including:

- Gifts valued at a dollar amount of $15k or less (for tax year 2018) to any one individual in a single calendar year – this is called the **annual gift exclusion amount**, it is indexed annually for inflation & it means that generally no tax payment or reporting is needed for gifts of that magnitude
- Gifts to a spouse
- Payment of tuition or medical expenses on someone else's behalf
- Charitable contributions
- Certain gifts to political organizations

It's important to understand that even if a gift is in excess of the $15k annual exclusion amount for gifts, there will likely be no cash gift tax to pay, but a gift tax return (IRS from 709) will need to be filed by April 15 of the year following the year when the gift was made. The return will report the fact that a gift exceeding the annual exclusion amount was made & will document a corresponding reduction of the much higher lifetime per person **combined / unified estate & gifts tax exemption** & that's where we get to the big tax reform changes that took place in this area.

The new law **doubled that lifetime exemption** & for tax year 2018 it has been locked in at a whopping **$11,180,000** (compared to $5,490,000 for 2017). The exemption amount is indexed annually for inflation.

Just to be clear – this means that any US person can give away over $11 million, either in form of gifts or bequests, without incurring any gift or estate taxes. For married couples, the combined exclusion is **over $22 million**. Now, whatever is in excess of this exclusion amount is taxed at 40%.

A similar (but separate!) exemption for the same amount is available for the **generation-skipping transfer tax (GSTT)**, so any utilization of this GSTT exemption has to be tracked separately from the unified gift & estate one. GSTT activity is reported on the same IRS forms 706 & 709, depending on the timing of the gift, i.e., during one's life or at death.

Like many other personal tax changes in the TCJA, these are temporary. For deaths & transfers after December 31, 2025, the exclusion amounts revert to pre-2018 levels with indexing applied. In other words, the 2026 exclusion will be roughly half of the 2025 amount.

According to the Joint Committee on Taxation, only the estates of the wealthiest 0.2% of Americans may owe estate tax.

If you are one of the wealthy taxpayers that may get affected by the estate tax, you may want to consider more generous giving to take advantage of the higher exemptions, while they are in effect. Also, please give me a call & teach me how to make a fortune!

Taxpayers often consider lifetime gifts with the goal of reducing or eliminating the estate tax that would otherwise be incurred at death.

Also, don't forget that when you make a gift, you are not only removing the value of the gifted asset from your taxable estate, but also any appreciation of that asset between the time of the gift & your death. So, by using some or all of the increased exemption amount to make additional tax-free lifetime gifts, individuals can transfer significant assets to others & shelter those transfers, along with any future appreciation in value, from taxation in their estate.

However, unlike assets transferred at death, lifetime gifts aren't entitled to a step-up in tax basis, but rather the donor's basis in the property carries over to the recipient. This may create a tax liability for the recipient of the gift if they choose to sell an appreciated gifted asset. Therefore, it makes sense to evaluate the potential estate tax savings versus the potential income tax costs to the recipient of the transferred asset.

Keep in mind that non-US citizens may be subject to US estate & gift taxation with respect to the value of their US 'situs' assets. **US situs assets** generally include real & tangible personal property located in the US, business assets located in the US & stock of US corporations. For non-residents, the estate tax exemption is **only $60k**, which is not applicable to the transfer of property by gift. This means that non-residents with US assets may face adverse US estate tax implications upon their death without careful planning. At the same time, the US has entered into estate & gift tax treaties with 16 jurisdictions, which can help reduce or eliminate double taxation & provide additional relief.

With respect to transfers at death, I won't say anything along the lines of 'use it while you can' – remember that **death is never a tax planning strategy worth considering**.

A couple of items worth mentioning in this area:

- The exemptions for estates & trusts remain at $100 (for a complex trust), $300 (for a simple trust) & $600 (for an estate)
- Non-US situs gifts (e.g., cash earned abroad) that US persons receive from non-residents are generally tax-free, but informational IRS form 3520 may need to be filed to report large gifts

4 / BUSINESS TAX

The biggest tax reform changes by far took place in the business / corporate space. As a country, we went from being a worldwide tax regime with one of the highest tax rates in the world to a quasi-territorial tax system with one of the lowest tax rates in the developed world. Wow.

Most business provisions went into effect on January 1, 2018, & unlike the personal changes we just discussed, most of the business ones are **permanent**. They are not scheduled to ever expire or sunset. Any future reversal or change to these newly enacted laws would require new legislation.

Businesses may be structured in a few different ways, but from a tax standpoint, they can generally be broken down into **corporations & pass-through entities**.

General corporations or C corporations (often abbreviated as 'C corps') are your classic US for-profit stock-based corporations. Usually, an 'Inc.' or 'Corp.' included in a company's legal name means it's a corporation, although it could be an S corporation (which is a type of pass-through entity), so always double-check to make sure. That's the entity form of choice for big businesses & publicly traded US companies. It's also pretty popular with startups seeking investors. C corporations are separate & distinct from their owners, not only on a legal level but also in the world of tax – they pay income tax on their own, on a corporate level, with no immediate impact to the owners, unless the owners receive payments from the corporation giving rise to taxes on their level (e.g., salaries, interest, dividends, or else). On the US federal level, C corps file their returns on IRS form 1120, which is due by April 15 of every year.

Pass-through entities are different – these are business structures where income gets allocated among the owners & income taxes are typically only levied at the owner level. Good examples of pass-through entities are partnerships, LLCs, S corporations & sole proprietorships. The way these businesses are taxed is referred to as flow-through taxation because generally the taxable income (or loss) of these entities is automatically transferred to the shareholder / owner level, every year. Some of these entities may have to file their own tax returns, but there will typically be no tax due with these returns, while tax will be due on the owners' returns for the share that 'flows through' to them. Partnerships file form 1065 & S corporations file form 1120-S, both due by March 15 of every year. Results for a sole proprietorship or a single member LLC generally land on the individual's tax return, on a Schedule C attached to Form 1040, to be exact.

In this chapter, I would like to talk about key tax reform changes affecting all businesses, followed by dedicated chapters on matters exclusively affecting corporations & pass-through entities. International provisions, compensation & benefits matters, as well as industry-specific tax implications will also be discussed later on in their respective chapters.

So here we go - below are the biggest tax reform items **affecting businesses of all kinds & shapes**.

IMMEDIATE EXPENSING / WRITE OFF

 IRC Sections 168(k) & 179

Typically, the cost of assets acquired for long-term business use gets capitalized & depreciated over time, which means the dollars spent don't get deducted immediately, but rather the deduction is taken over time, as the asset is used, based on specific tax rules.

Bonus depreciation rules in Section 168(k) & the Section 179 deduction are both designed to accelerate these deductions for tax purposes & have been around for a while but were greatly expanded by the TCJA.

Under previous tax rules, the bonus depreciation deduction was limited to 50% of eligible new property. Tax reform extends & modifies bonus depreciation to allow businesses to immediately deduct 100% of eligible property placed-in-service after September 27, 2017, & before January 1, 2023, & for certain property with longer production periods, the 100% bonus depreciation is extended through the end of 2023.

Bonus depreciation is available for qualifying property, which is generally property with a depreciable recovery period (i.e., life) of 20 years or less. Eligible property has been expanded to include used property, film, television & stage equipment.

Section 179 allows a taxpayer to immediately expense the cost of qualifying property, rather than via depreciation deductions. TCJA increased the maximum amount a taxpayer could deduct per year for property placed in service after December 31, 2017, from $500k to $1 million. The phase-out threshold has also been increased.

Qualifying property for Section 179 expensing has been expanded & now includes furnishings for lodgings (e.g., furniture, refrigerators, appliances), as well as new roofs, HVAC systems, fire & security alarms for commercial buildings.

The expensing provisions are clearly designed to stimulate the economy by encouraging tax favorable acquisitions of business assets & spending on infrastructure & equipment. The next few years might be a good time to buy that new amazing equipment you've been dreaming of, but only for your business use, of course!

ACCOUNTING METHODS

 IRC Section 448

The act expanded the list of taxpayers that are eligible to use the **cash method of accounting** by allowing taxpayers that have average annual gross receipts of $25 million or less in the three prior tax years to use the cash method. The $25 million gross receipts threshold will be indexed for inflation after 2018. Under the provision, the cash method of accounting may be used by taxpayers, that satisfy the gross-receipts test, regardless of whether the purchase, production, or sale of merchandise is an income-producing factor.

The current law exceptions from the use of the accrual method otherwise remain the same, so qualified personal service corporations, partnerships without C corporation partners, S corporations & other pass-through entities continue to be allowed to use the cash method without regard to the gross receipts test, as long as the use of that method clearly reflects income.

Taxpayers that meet the gross receipts test will not be required to account for inventories under Section 471 & will be exempt from the uniform capitalization (UniCap) rules of Section 263A. The exemptions from the UniCap rules that are not based on gross receipts are retained in the law.

REVENUE RECOGNITION

 IRC Section 451(b)

The act requires accrual method taxpayers subject to the all events test to recognize items of gross income for tax purposes in the year in which they recognize the income on their applicable financial statement (generally, an audited financial statement). The act provides an exception for taxpayers without an applicable financial statement.

The provision also codifies the one-year deferral of advance payments & the definition of advanced payments.

INTEREST DEDUCTION LIMITATION

 IRC Section 163(j)

Under the new law, the deduction for business interest is generally **limited to 30%** of the taxpayer's adjusted taxable income.

For these purposes, business interest means any interest paid or accrued on indebtedness properly allocable to a trade or business.

For tax years 2018 through 2021, the computation of **adjusted taxable income** should approximately reflect business earnings before interest, taxes, depreciation & amortization (**EBITDA**). For tax years beginning after 2021, the adjusted taxable income would then be the approximate earnings before interest & taxes (**EBIT**). As a result, adjusted taxable income should decrease, ultimately reducing the maximum amount of deductible business interest expense.

Businesses will be able to **carry forward any unused business interest expense indefinitely**.

Taxpayers that have average annual gross receipts of $25 million or less in the three prior tax years are exempt. The limitation will also not apply to any real property development, construction, acquisition, conversion, rental, operation, management, leasing, or brokerage trade or business. Farming businesses are allowed to elect out of the limitation.

NET OPERATING LOSSES (NOLs)

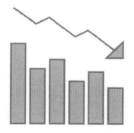

 IRC Section 172

Under old law business net operating losses (or NOLs for short) could generally be carried back two years & carried forward 20 years to offset taxable income.

Tax reform **repealed the two-year carryback** provision for losses arising in tax years 2018 & beyond. On the bright side - NOLs may now be carried forward **indefinitely** rather than for only 20 years.

The TCJA also limits the utilization of NOLs. Starting with tax year 2018, businesses may no longer use NOLs to offset all of their taxable income in subsequent years.

The NOL deduction got **limited to 80% of taxable income** (determined without regard to the new 20% pass-thru deduction). In other words, business owners may no longer use NOLs to reduce their tax liability to zero in a profitable tax year.

Here's an example:

Fabio owns a business that recorded a net loss of $100 in 2018. The business does better in 2019, bringing in a $100 profit.

Under prior law, Fabio could deduct the 2018 loss in 2019, fully eliminating the tax liability.

Post tax reform, Fabio may only deduct $80 (80%

of $100) & will still need to pay taxes on 20 dollars of income in 2019. The disallowed $20 NOL can be carried forward to next year & beyond.

A couple of exceptions:

- Farming businesses are still allowed a two-year NOL carryback
- Property & casualty insurance companies are exempt from the new rules & continue to use the old rules

LIKE-KIND EXCHANGES (LKEs)

 IRC Section 1031

A like-kind exchange (LKE) under US tax law, also known as a Section 1031 exchange, is a transaction or series of transactions that allows for the disposal of an asset & the acquisition of another replacement asset without generating a current tax liability from the sale of the asset. New property receives the basis of the old property, effectively deferring any taxable gain or loss until the new replacement property is ultimately sold or disposed of.

Under the TCJA, like-kind exchanges (LKEs) under Section 1031 will be **limited to exchanges of real estate property** that is not primarily held for sale.

This provision generally applies to exchanges completed after December 31, 2017. However, an exception is provided for any exchange where the property disposed of by the taxpayer in the exchange was disposed of on or before December 31, 2017, or the property received by the taxpayer in the exchange was received on or before that date, i.e., if one side of your LKE transaction occurred in 2017 & the other in 2018, you may still apply LKE rules.

ENTERTAINMENT EXPENSES

 IRC Section 274

The new law fully **disallows** any deduction for:

- Activities generally considered to be entertainment, amusement, or recreation
- Membership dues for any club organized for business, pleasure, recreation, or other social purposes
- A facility or portion thereof used in connection with any of the above items

One of the exceptions from the rule is for expenses for recreation, social, or similar activities primarily for the benefit of the taxpayer's employees, other than highly compensated employees, which means that office holiday parties & similar events continue to be fully deductible.

TRANSPORTATION FRINGE BENEFITS

 IRC Section 274

The act **disallows** a deduction for expenses associated with providing any qualified transportation fringe to employees of the taxpayer & any expense incurred for providing transportation for commuting between the employee's residence & place of employment, or any related payment / reimbursement of such, except as necessary for ensuring the safety of an employee.

MEALS

 IRC Section 274

Under the new law, businesses are **still generally able to deduct 50%** of the food & beverage expenses associated with operating their trade or business, e.g., meals consumed by employees when traveling for work, or meals with clients. No changes with respect to these.

Under old law, companies were getting a full deduction for any meals provided for the convenience of employer (e.g., meals served at meetings at the office), occasional meals provided to personnel, overtime meals, water, coffee & snacks at the office, sometimes referred to as 'internal' or 'on-site' meals. The new law **expands the 50% limitation** to all these types of meals & snacks starting in 2018 & makes them **non-deductible at all after 2025.**

RESEARCH & DEVELOPMENT

 IRC Section 174

TCJA **repeals the options to expense R&D** costs or defer them over a period of 60 or more months. Instead, amounts defined as specified research or experimental expenditures must be capitalized & **amortized ratably over a five-year period**. Specified research or experimental expenditures that are attributable to research that is conducted outside of the United States must be capitalized & amortized ratably over a 15-year period. The provision applies to research or experimental expenditures paid after December 31, 2021.

The research tax credit under IRC Section 51 is retained.

Inventors with self-made intellectual property such as inventions, patents & designs may not enjoy lower tax rates like before. The Tax Cuts & Jobs

Act eliminates the ability to consider self-made property as capital assets, which are subject to the lower capital gains rate of 20%. Rather, self-made property is now taxed as ordinary income. This may transform how patented assets are sold & impact deals made across the technology space.

LOCAL LOBBYING

 IRC Section 162(e)

Old law permitted taxpayers to deduct lobbying expenses for local lobbying as ordinary & necessary business expenses.

The Act **repealed** Sections 162(e)(2) & (e)(7), thereby prohibiting deductions for lobbying expenses for legislation before local government bodies (including Indian tribal governments).

OTHER BUSINESS PROVISIONS

DEDUCTIONS FOR FINES & PENALTIES

The Act **expands the disallowance of deductions for fines & penalties** paid to government entities to also include amounts related to restitution, remediation or correction of noncompliance with any law, with exceptions & additionally, provides that:

- similar payments made to certain nongovernmental regulatory entities may now also be denied
- government agencies are now required to report to the IRS & the taxpayer the amount of each settlement agreement or order where the amount is at least $600

SEXUAL HARASSMENT

The new law denies a business deduction for any settlement, payout or attorney fees related to sexual harassment or abuse if the settlement or payment is subject to a nondisclosure agreement (NDA). This rule is effective for amounts paid or incurred after the enactment date, December 22, 2017.

DEPRECIATION OF LUXURY AUTOMOBILES

The Act increases the Section 280F deduction limitations to:

- $10k in the first year
- $16k in the second year
- $9.6k in the third year
- $5.76k in each succeeding year

KEY REPEALED / ADJUSTED PROVISIONS

- Domestic production activity deduction (DPAD) under Section 199 was repealed
- Rehabilitation tax credit – the Act repeals the 10% credit for pre-1936 buildings but keeps the 20% credit for expenses to rehabilitate certain historic structures
- Orphan drug credit rate reduced from 50% to 25%
- Repeals the deduction for employee achievement awards in the form of cash, cash equivalents, gift certificates, vacations, meals, lodging, tickets to events, stocks, bonds, securities, or other similar items

SIGNIFICANT RETAINED PROVISIONS

- Research credit
- New markets tax credit

- Work opportunity tax credit
- Credit for employer-provided childcare
- Disabled access credit
- Credit for FICA taxes on tips
- American Samoa economic development credit
- Enhanced oil recovery (EOR) credit
- Renewable electricity production tax credit (PTC)
- Percentage depletion allowance deduction
- Credit for production from advanced nuclear power facilities
- Business energy investment tax credit (ITC)
- Unused business credits carryovers
- Deductibility of law firm expense advances made on behalf of clients in the context of contingent fee cases

5 / C CORPORATIONS

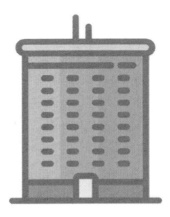

Stock corporations, C corporations, or just corporations is what most people mean when they are talking big business. A C corporation files a federal tax return on IRS form 1120 & pays tax on the corporate level. Shareholders of corporations are subject to potential tax on dividends or distributions they receive from the company, which is why operating via a corporation is often referred to as creating 'double taxation.' However, this may not be a big deal for companies that do not intend to pay dividends or those with plans to reinvest any earnings back into the business. Also, if a corporation is paying a salary to its owner or pays him or her as a consultant (both scenarios are generally permitted), then the corporation gets a deduction & the owner includes the payment as income on their return, so no double taxation occurs in these instances.

Most public companies & high-growth startups are organized as corporations, often registered in Delaware, a state known for its business-friendly & predictable corporate governance environment.

A **Professional or Personal Service Corporation (PSC)** is a business entity formed according to state law for the purpose of providing services in a specific professional practice area, typically used by licensed professionals such as attorneys, architects, engineers, public accountants & physicians. PSCs are taxed like C corps.

A **Benefit corporation or B Corp** is a type of for-profit corporate entity, authorized by 33 US states & the District of Columbia that includes positive impact on society, workers, the community & the environment, in addition to profit, as its legally defined goals. Benefit corporation status only affects requirements of corporate purpose, accountability & transparency. Everything else regarding corporation laws & tax law remains the same, therefore benefit corporations are taxed just like C corps.

Don't confuse C corporations with S corporations, which are taxed more like partnerships, in a flow-through manner. An S corporation actually starts off as a classic C corporation but files an election with the IRS to be treated as an S corp. We will discuss S corps taxation in more detail in the next chapter dedicated to pass-through entities.

The various business tax provisions I went over in the previous chapter apply to all businesses, including corporations. The items discussed in this chapter are specific to corporations only.

THE NEW 21% RATE

 IRC Section 11

Under prior law, corporations were taxed based on a graduated rate structure with a top rate of 35%. The TCJA eliminated that system & replaced it with a **permanent flat 21% corporate income tax rate** which went into effect on January 1, 2018.

CORPORATE AMT

 IRC Section 55

The new law **repeals the corporate alternative minimum tax (AMT)** for good, effective January 1, 2018.

However, corporations with prior year AMT credits will be able to carry forward the credit & offset it against the corporation's regular tax liability & may even be eligible to receive a cash refund in years 2018 through 2021 for a portion of the AMT credits that exceeded the regular liability, subject to some limitations.

DIVIDENDS RECEIVED DEDUCTION

 IRC Section 243

The dividends received deduction, or DRD, is a tax deduction that C corporations receive on the dividends distributed to them by other companies whose stock they own. The higher the corporation's equity interest in a dividend-paying company, the higher is the DRD.

Tax reform changed the portions of the dividends that are exempt from tax via the DRD as presented in the following table:

Ownership %	DRD (old law)	DRD (new law)
< 20%	70%	50%
20 - 80%	80%	60%
> 80%	100%	100%

These unfavorable changes are meant as a compensation for the reduced corporate tax rates.

CAPITAL CONTRIBUTIONS

 IRC Section 118

Contributions to capital of a corporation are generally excluded from gross income.

The TCJA modified Section 118 to provide that the term 'contributions to capital' does not include:

- Any contribution in aid of construction or any other contribution as a customer or potential customer &
- Any contribution by any governmental entity or civic group (other than a contribution made by a shareholder as such)

S TO C CORPORATE CONVERSIONS

After the huge tax cut that C corporations got, some S corps may conclude that it would be more advantageous for them to be taxed as C corps. Luckily the 'conversion' process is pretty simple – with majority shareholder consent, an S corporation may revoke its election to be taxed under Subchapter S & revert to the default C status.

The new law permits an eligible terminated S corporation to take a Section 481(a) adjustment over six years to capture any accounting changes needed as part of the conversion, e.g., required changes from the cash method to the accrual method.

Additionally, the Act treats a portion of dividends paid by an eligible terminated S corporation after its post-termination transition period as coming from its accumulated adjustments account, which would generally be tax-free to the shareholders.

6 / PASS-THROUGHS

Many American businesses are set up as **pass-through or unincorporated entities** & include:

- A **sole proprietorship**, which is the simplest business form & often requires no formal registration. A sole proprietor is just somebody operating under their own name, or possibly under a DBA (doing business as) name. Sole proprietors do not file separate tax returns, but business income & expenses are reported on their individual returns on a Schedule C attached to a federal IRS form

1040. Typically, an LLC (Limited Liability Company) with just one owner (often referred to as a single member LLC or SMLLC) is a disregarded entity (DRE) for tax purposes, so a SMLLC is effectively just a sole proprietorship with a formal state registration & a registered business name. People often choose to register an LLC when they operate on their own to get a certain level of liability protection & to have a more sophisticated business image. From a tax perspective, a SMLLC is generally taxed the same way as a sole proprietor without any registration, at least on the federal level. Some states, like California & New York, may impose LLC fees

- A **partnership**, which represents an association or an agreement (which doesn't necessarily need to be in writing) of two or more persons to carry on a business or venture together & these can take different legal forms like limited (LP) or general partnerships (GP), or multi-member LLCs. A partnership files a separate return, IRS form 1065 & passes income & losses to the partners who are responsible for reporting these results on their individual or business tax returns & paying any applicable taxes

- A **Limited Liability Company (LLC)**, which is a flexible / hybrid kind of entity that depending on its ownership structure offers the options to be taxed as a sole proprietor, a partnership or even a corporation (if a special election is made on IRS form 8832). LLCs that elected corporate treatment follow tax rules for C corporations, not pass-through businesses

- An **S Corporation** is a corporation with tax treatment similar to a partnership. S corporation status is achieved by registering a general corporation & then electing S corporation treatment on a timely filed IRS form 2553. An S Corporation files a federal form 1120-S, which passes most items of income or loss to shareholders who are responsible for reporting that information on their individual tax returns. S corps have a bunch of special limitations & rules, e.g., they are not allowed to have foreign shareholders or more than 100 shareholders in total, plus if a shareholder provides services to the S corporation, he/she must receive an adequate & reasonable salary for these services

As you learned from the previous chapter, the new tax law now provides for a flat 21% tax rate for corporations. You can imagine how this drastic tax cut (from the old 35%) could create issues without changes to pass-through taxation. For a long time, taxpayers have been incentivized to set up businesses as pass-through entities, because in such a structure income is not taxed at the entity level & is only taxed once on the individual level, where tax rates were historically lower than corporate rates for many taxpayers.

Although the Tax Cuts & Jobs Act did cut individual tax rates, the cut was not nearly as dramatic as the corporate tax cut. So, what solution did Congress come up with to bring some parity between the now much lower corporate rates & those applicable to pass-through income? They introduced IRC Section 199A, which provides for a special deduction of up to 20% from qualified pass-through income, in order to indirectly bring the effective rate applicable to business income lower.

20% PASS-THROUGH DEDUCTION

 IRC Section 199A

Business owners who qualify can deduct up to 20% of their net business income from their income taxes, reducing their effective income tax rate by 20% (meaning that if your rate was 30% before applying the deduction, it would be 24% when the deduction is factored in). This deduction is available starting with tax year 2018 & is scheduled to expire at the end of 2025 unless extended by Congress. So, another temporary provision, similar to the individual & wealth transfer tax rules we discussed earlier.

It sounds easy but can get tricky since the deduction is subject to a number of limitations & restrictions. Let's get into some details & start with a few definitions.

Qualified business income (QBI) is generally the net income from your business. QBI excludes capital gains (short or long-term), dividend income, interest income, wages paid to S corporation shareholders or that you earn as an employee, guaranteed payments to partners or LLC members, or income generated outside the US. QBI is determined on a per business basis. So a taxpayer that owns more than one profitable business could have several buckets of QBI.

Qualified property means tangible property subject to depreciation & available for use in your business at the end of the tax year. The property must be used in the production of QBI.

A **specified service trade or business** or **personal service business** is any business involving the performance of services in the fields of health, law, consulting, athletics, financial services, brokerage services, or 'any trade or business where the principal asset of such trade or business is the reputation or skill of one or more of its employees or owners.' In other words, if the success of your business depends on you & not on something that you sell, you have a specified business (except for engineering & architecture services, which were specifically excluded).

There are also two important thresholds that will determine the allowable deduction level & any applicable limitations:

1st threshold level – taxable income of less than $157.5k for single filers / $315k for joint filers

2nd threshold level - taxable income of more than $207.5k for single filers / $415k for joint filers

If your taxable income falls **below the 1st threshold** level then you get to take the full 20% deduction on your QBI pass-through income, no questions asked. It doesn't even matter if you are in a 'specified' business category defined above.

If your taxable income is above **the 2nd threshold level** & you are in the 'specified service trade or business' category (e.g., a law firm), you will get **no deduction at all**. All other businesses may still get a deduction, but it will be limited (and could be even eliminated) based on the **wage/capital limitation** that we will discuss below.

If your taxable income is **between the two thresholds** (the phase-out range), you are eligible for a partial tax benefit. It's available regardless of the nature of the business, but the amount of business income eligible for the deduction phases out in a complicated way.

The **wage/capital limitation** for the deduction is:

- the greater of 50% of wages with respect to your trade or business, or
- the sum of 25% of wages + 2.5% of the unadjusted basis, immediately after

acquisition, of all **qualified property**

The addition of qualified property to the formula was designed to accommodate businesses which rely on the acquisition of capital assets, like real estate companies.

Below is an example of how the wage/capital limitation works in practice:

- you have $10k in wages & you buy equipment worth $300k & place it in service during the year
- accordingly, 50% of wages equals $5k
- per the second part of the formula: 25% of wages + 2.5% of the unadjusted basis of the equipment will give us $10k
- since the greater of the two amounts is $10k, that's what we will be using to figure your deduction

This was, of course, an illustration of an asset-heavy enterprise. If your business had no property or your wages were higher, then the 50% of wages would likely be your limitation.

Business owners compare their resulting wage/capital limitation amount to a straight 20% percent of their QBI & may deduct the smaller of the two amounts.

No matter which variation of the formula applies in your case, your deduction may not exceed your taxable income for the year (adjusted by net capital gain). If the net amount of your QBI is a loss, you'll just carry it forward as a loss to the following tax year.

The pass-through deduction reduces taxable income on your individual return. It does not change how you calculate your taxable income within the business. Business expenses remain deductible & all other business rules still apply.

EXCESS BUSINESS LOSSES

 IRC Section 461(l)

Business losses of taxpayers other than C corporations are only permitted in the current year to the extent that they do not exceed the sum of:

- taxpayer's gross income &
- $500k for joint filers or $250k for other taxpayers

Excess businesses losses will be disallowed & added to the taxpayer's net operating loss (NOL) carryforward.

Here's an example:

During 2018 Jaime Vegas is single & has $1 million of gross income & $1.5 million of deductions from his bodega in Union City, NJ. His excess business loss is $250k calculated as follows:

- $1.5 million of gross deductions **less** the sum of gross income plus the applicable limitation, $1.5m − ($1m + $250k) = $250k of excess losses

Jaime must treat his excess business loss as an NOL carryover to 2019. For a detailed discussion of the NOL rules, please refer to chapter 3.

For pass-through entities, this limitation is applied at the partner / shareholder level.

This rule expires / sunsets at the end of 2025.

PARTNERSHIP PROVISIONS

TECHNICAL TERMINATIONS

 IRC Section 708(b)(1)(B)

The Act repealed the Section 708(b)(1)(B) rule that terminated a partnership if, within any 12-month period, there was a sale or exchange of 50% or more of the total interest in partnership capital & profits. The provision does not change the rule in Section 708(b)(1)(A) that a partnership is considered to be terminated if no part of any business, financial operation, or venture of the partnership continues to be carried on by any of its partners in a partnership.

GAIN ON SALE OF PARTNERSHIP INTEREST BY A FOREIGN PARTNER

 IRC Sections 862(c) & 1446

For sales & exchanges on or after November 27, 2017, gain or loss from the sale or exchange of a partnership interest is deemed effectively connected with a US trade or business to the extent that the transferor would have had effectively connected gain or loss had the partnership sold all of its assets at fair market value as of the date of the sale or exchange.

PARTNERSHIP 'SUBSTANTIAL BUILT-IN LOSS' MODIFIED

 IRC Section 743(d)

The new tax law expands the definition of a substantial built-in loss for partnerships & says that such loss now also exists if the transferee partner is allocated a loss in excess of $250k upon a hypothetical disposition by the partnership of all partnership's assets in a fully taxable transaction for cash equal to the assets' fair market value, immediately after the transfer of the partnership interest. This provision applies to transfers of partnership interests occurring after December 31, 2017.

CHARITABLE CONTRIBUTIONS & FOREIGN TAXES IN PARTNER'S SHARE OF LOSS

 IRC Section 704(d)

For 2018 & beyond, charitable contributions & taxes paid or accrued to foreign countries or US possessions are taken into account when determining the amount of a partner's loss.

7 / INTERNATIONAL

Historically, prior to tax reform, both US individuals & businesses were generally taxed on their worldwide income, but with important exceptions. For example, active business income earned by foreign subsidiaries was generally not subject to US tax until actually repatriated to its US parent or shareholders. Some US-headquartered multinational businesses were employing global tax planning strategies designed to centralize international earnings offshore (ideally in low tax jurisdictions) & thereby defer US tax on those foreign earnings, often indefinitely.

Estimates vary, but US companies were thought to have at least $2 trillion of foreign earnings held in cash, cash equivalents & illiquid assets overseas that have not been subject to US tax.

The main tool historically available for US companies to avoid double taxation once the money came onshore was the foreign tax credit (FTC).

A couple of important terms that we will be referring to in this chapter:

- **Controlled Foreign Corporation (CFC)** is any foreign corporation in which more than 50% of the total value of the stock is owned directly, indirectly or constructively by US shareholders on any day during the taxable year of the corporation
- **Specified Foreign Corporation (SFC)** is any **CFC** or any foreign corporation which has at least one US corporate shareholder
- **Subpart F** refers to a set of provisions designed to limit the deferral of US taxation of certain types of income earned by **CFCs**

Tax reform made dramatic changes to the rules governing international taxation. Most provisions are focused on making US companies more competitive & bringing more investment into the United States, but the new rules also attempt to combat base erosion & profit shifting through a set of brand new anti-abuse rules.

PARTICIPATION EXEMPTION

 IRC Section 245A

Probably the biggest update to the US international tax regime is its move from a worldwide system of taxation closer to a territorial one, achieved primarily by letting domestic corporations exclude from their US taxable income the foreign-source portion of dividends they receive from their foreign subsidiaries via a dividends received deduction (DRD). A 100% DRD is allowed for dividends received from foreign corporations in which the US corporation owns a 10% or more stake, effectively creating a **full participation exemption**, similar to what is offered in many other counties around the world. A couple of important notes on it though:

- This exemption is only available to C corporations & not available to individuals or unincorporated US shareholders of foreign corporations

- The exemption applies only if the stock of the foreign corporation had been held for more than a year
- Not allowed for any 'hybrid dividends' which means dividends that were allowed as a deduction to a CFC
- No foreign tax credit (FTC) will be allowed for any portion of the distribution that is already exempt under this provision

MANDATORY REPATRIATION TAX

 IRC Section 965

As part of the transition to the new participation exemption system outlined above, the new law mandates US shareholders to pay a one-time transition tax (sometimes referred to as the 'toll tax') on their accumulated foreign profits under the new IRC Section 965, which requires all US shareholders that own 10% or more of certain foreign corporations (SFCs as defined above, to be more specific) to include on their 2017 tax returns their share of their foreign corporations' foreign income on which US taxation was previously deferred, which is effectively the sum of any un-repatriated foreign earnings sitting abroad, i.e., the trillions of dollars kept offshore to avoid US tax under the old deferral regime are now subject to this one-time toll tax. The amount deemed repatriated is the greater of the accumulated foreign earnings as of November 2, 2017, or December 31, 2017. These two dates are referred to as the 'measurement dates.'

Earnings & profits (E&P) of the foreign corporations is what's used to calculate the inclusion. E&P data can generally be located on IRS forms 5471 filed for the corporation, on Schedules H & J of that form, to be exact.

A portion of that pro rata share of foreign earnings is deductible via a special dividends received deduction (DRD). The mechanics are somewhat unusual: the total deduction allowed is a 'plug' amount necessary to produce an effective 15.5% rate of tax on foreign earnings held in form of cash or cash equivalents & an 8% tax on all other earnings. The taxpayer can elect to pay the calculated tax liability over a period of eight years.

In addition to the DRD, Section 965 offers a number of provisions that may soften the impact of the mandatory repatriation tax. Previously taxed income (PTI), such as Subpart F income picked up in earlier periods, reduces the amount subject to inclusion & deficit-netting rules at the CFC, shareholder & affiliated or consolidated group levels may significantly reduce the repatriation inclusion.

To put the netting part in perspective – imagine that you own two foreign corporations, one has positive accumulated E&P of $100 & the other one has negative cumulative E&P (a deficit) of $100. In this scenario, you will have no Section 965 inclusion as the net E&P is zero.

Similarly, if the foreign corporations have no profits or are generating losses, there will be no 'toll tax.'

Taxpayers may apply NOLs & claim a foreign tax credit (which is adjusted to reflect the DRD reduction).

For S corporation shareholders, special rules apply that effectively permit indefinite deferral of the repatriation tax until the S corporation is sold or liquidated.

Once this tax is paid, the cash can be brought back to USA tax-free as previously taxed income (PTI) &

put to work here to create jobs & make America great again, which was the whole point of this tax.

GLOBAL INTANGIBLE LOW-TAXED INCOME (GILTI)

 IRC Section 951A

GILTI is a new type of Subpart F income created by the TCJA. For tax years 2018 & beyond, Section 951A requires US shareholders of CFCs to include their share of GILTI in current income, similar to other Subpart F inclusions. Generally speaking, GILTI means the excess of a US shareholder's share of CFC income over the shareholder's deemed 10% return on the CFC's tangible assets for the year. GILTI does not include effectively connected income (ECI) unless subject to reduced tax under a treaty, other Subpart F income, income subject to high tax rates in a foreign country, related-party dividends, or foreign oil & gas income. Income qualifying for certain exceptions from Subpart F can increase GILTI.

An indirect foreign tax credit is allowed for taxes paid on GILTI, but the credit is limited to 80% of the foreign taxes, has a separate limitation basket & cannot be carried back or forward to other years. For US shareholders that are C corporations (other than REITs or RICs), a deduction is allowed for up to 50% of the GILTI inclusion amount, resulting in an effective tax rate of 10.5% for GILTI. The deduction decreases to 37.5% of GILTI for tax years 2026 & beyond.

Individual shareholders are not entitled to the GILTI deduction, the foreign tax credit & the reduced 21% corporate tax rate on GILTI income, but they may get some of these corporate benefits by filing a Section 962 election, which is an election by an individual to be treated as a corporation for Subpart F purposes, that will generally result in an individual shareholder getting the indirect foreign tax credit & the 21% corporate rate, but not the GILTI deduction.

The tax on GILTI is intended to ensure US taxpayers pay at least some US tax on low-taxed or untaxed income of a CFC, above a nominal return on a CFC's fixed assets, effectively establishing a minimum tax on profits in foreign subsidiaries.

For a corporate US parent, all this ultimately means

that if GILTI is subject to non-US tax at a minimum rate of 13.125%, no further US tax should be due (i.e., 13.125% @ 80% = the 10.5% effective US tax rate after taking into account the 50% GILTI deduction from the income taxed at 21%).

For years 2026 & beyond, the GILTI effective tax rate increases to 13.125% & the foreign tax rate of the CFC required to pay no additional US tax under the GILTI regime increases to 16.406%.

So, GILTI, despite its unabbreviated name, has little to do with what is traditionally considered income from intangibles, while the abbreviation speaks for itself.

FOREIGN-DERIVED INTANGIBLE INCOME (FDII)

 IRC Section 250

Presumably intended to encourage domestic corporations to develop intangibles in the US, the Act creates the new Foreign-Derived Intangible Income (FDII) bucket of specially treated income. In broad terms, the FDII of a domestic corporation is the deemed intangible income that the domestic corporation earns from making sales of property to non-US persons for foreign use & for providing services to persons or with respect to property located outside the US. The new law provides for a deduction of up to 37.5% of a domestic corporation's FDII for the year, resulting in an effective federal tax rate of 13.125% on such income (compared to the new standard 21% corporate tax rate). FDII is somewhat similar to GILTI (discussed above), but instead of being punitive, it creates a bucket of income that is taxed at a reduced rate. FDII is arrived at by calculating a corporation's deemed intangible income from serving foreign markets after allowing for a 10% return on the corporation's depreciable business assets. FDII does not include Subpart F income, dividends, or GILTI.

The deduction decreases to 21.875% of FDII in 2026, producing an effective tax rate of 16.406% for tax years 2026 & beyond.

The FDII deduction is a great incentive for US corporations which are light on fixed assets & sell globally, such as companies in the services or technology sectors.

SUBPART F UPDATES

 ### IRC Sections 951, 958 & 965

The TCJA changes the ownership attribution rules so that a US corporation can be treated as constructively owning stock held by its foreign shareholder. This change, however, only applies for purposes of determining whether a foreign corporation is a CFC. The Subpart F income that a US shareholder is required to include in gross income continues to be determined based on direct or indirect ownership of the CFC.

The Act expands the definition of US shareholder to include any US person who owns 10% of the total value of shares of all classes of stock of a foreign corporation. Under prior law, the determination of whether a US person was a US shareholder was based on the ownership of 10% of the voting power of all classes of stock of a foreign corporation.

The Act eliminates the requirement that a corporation must be controlled for an uninterrupted period of 30 days before Subpart F inclusions apply.

The TCJA also repeals the treatment of foreign base company oil-related income as Subpart F & repeals certain Subpart F provisions associated with foreign base company shipping income.

BASE EROSION & ANTI-ABUSE TAX (BEAT)

 IRC Section 59A

Base erosion & profit shifting (or BEPS) refers to corporate tax planning strategies used by multinational companies that artificially shift profits from higher-tax locations to lower-tax locations, thus 'eroding' the tax-base of the higher-tax locations. These structures are also known as BEPS tools or BEPS schemes.

As its name suggests, the BEAT of the new Section 59A is meant to punch base erosion. BEAT applies to corporate taxpayers (other than REITs, RICs & S corporations) that are part of a group with average gross receipts of $500 million over the preceding three years & a 3% or higher base erosion percentage. ECI (effectively connected income) of foreign affiliates is included for purposes of the gross receipts threshold. The base erosion percentage basically means the ratio of deductions for base erosion payments (i.e., deductible payments to a foreign related party) to total deductions. Operating **like a minimum tax**, BEAT applies if a corporation's base erosion payments reduce its US tax liability to less than 10% of its 'modified taxable income' (this rate goes up to 12.5% in 2026). For affiliated groups that include a bank or securities dealer, a 2% base erosion percentage threshold applies & the applicable BEAT rate is 11% (13.5% for tax years after 2025).

Base erosion payments do not include amounts paid for costs of goods sold (unless paid to an expatriated entity or foreign members of its expanded affiliated group), for services eligible for the services cost method under Section 482 & with no markup component & for certain qualified derivative payments made in the ordinary course of business.

There are concerns that the BEAT may be in violation to World Trade Organization rules & nondiscrimination provisions of existing US income tax treaties & that other countries could enact retaliatory tax laws.

ANTI-HYBRID PROVISIONS

 IRC Section 267A

A hybrid entity is an entity that is subject to corporate income tax in one national jurisdiction, but that qualifies for tax transparent (or disregarded) treatment in another, typically resulting in tax savings.

The Act **denies deductions for related-party interest or royalties paid or accrued in hybrid transactions or to or from hybrid entities**. Specifically, any interest or royalty paid or accrued to a related party is not deductible for US tax purposes to the extent the amount is either not included in the income of the foreign related party or is deductible from the taxable income of the related party in such related party's tax jurisdiction as a result of the hybrid nature of the payment or of the related-party entity.

A hybrid transaction is any transaction, series of transactions, agreement or instrument under which a payment treated as a payment of interest or royalties for US tax purposes is not so treated for relevant foreign tax purposes.

The new rule does not apply to payments that are included in the income of a US shareholder under Subpart F.

FOREIGN TAX CREDIT (FTC) CHANGES

Apart from foreign tax credit rules impacted by new international provisions discussed above, the Act makes several changes to other existing rules.

The indirect or deemed paid **Section 902 foreign tax credit is repealed**. However, Section 960 is amended to preserve the treatment of a corporate US shareholder as paying foreign taxes attributable to its Subpart F inclusions & to PTI distributions, including distributions through tiered CFCs.

A US corporate shareholder of a passive foreign investment company treated as a **qualified electing fund will also be treated as paying foreign taxes** on PTI distributions of the qualified electing fund if the shareholder meets the ownership requirements of former Section 902.

The Act also adds a **new foreign tax credit limitation category** to Section 904(d) for non-passive income of a foreign branch.

OTHER INTERNATIONAL PROVISIONS

Additionally, the TCJA:

- Provides **further limitations to income shifting through intangible transfers** by making it clear that workforce in place, goodwill & going concern value are considered intangibles

- Modifies Section 963(b) **rules for sourcing income** from the sale or exchange of inventory property
- Restricts the application of the **qualified dividend rules** for surrogate foreign corporations
- Restricts **exceptions for certain insurance companies** under the passive foreign investment company (PFIC) rules
- Requires members of a US-affiliated group to **allocate interest expense based on the adjusted tax basis of assets**, rather than fair market value (FMV)
- Increases the **penalty for failing to timely file IRS Form 5472**, information return of a 25% foreign-owned US corporation, from $10k to $25k

8 / COMPENSATION & BENEFITS

Tax reform introduced some meaningful changes & new rules in the area of employee compensation & benefits. Discussed below are some of the key provisions in this space.

EMPLOYER CREDIT FOR PAID FAMILY & MEDICAL LEAVE

 IRC Section 45S

The Act introduces a **temporary employer credit** that allows eligible employers to claim a general business tax credit equal to 12.5% of qualifying employee wages paid during the period in which the employee is on family & medical leave, as long as the program's payment rate is 50% of the employee's normal wages. The maximum leave period that qualifies for the credit for a tax year is 12 weeks.

The credit is increased by 0.25% (but not above 25% in aggregate) for each percentage point by which the program's payment rate exceeds 50% of the employee's normal wages.

Qualifying employees are those with at least one year of service & wages that do not exceed $72k (as indexed for inflation in 2018).

Employers that provide all qualifying full-time employees at least two weeks of annual paid family & medical leave & provide part-time employees an amount of leave on a pro rata basis qualify for the credit.

The credit is available for wages paid in calendar years 2018 & 2019 only.

EXECUTIVE COMPENSATION

 IRC Section 162(m)

Section 162(m) is not new & it previously limited the ability of publicly traded companies to deduct remuneration for services to a $1 million maximum, if paid to the principal executive officer & the next four highest-paid executives (other than the principal financial officer, such as the CFO). Performance-based compensation, commissions, & other limited exceptions were not included in the total amount that was subject to the limit.

The Act, however, **expands the application of this limitation** in several important ways:

- More companies could now be subject to the rule, including all SEC-registrars, foreign corporations traded through American depository receipts (ADR) & even certain large private corporations
- It now applies to a broader group of people: the 'covered employees' for any year now include the CEO, CFO & the three other highest paid people. Any person who was a covered employee in 2017 remains a covered employee forever. Any beneficiaries

> of covered employees are treated as covered employees

- Performance-based compensation & post-termination items, including severance & other parachute payments, are now also included in the amount that is subject to the limitation
- A transition rule allows a public company to continue using old rules if the company has a written, binding contract in effect on November 2, 2017, that was not modified later

As a result, beginning in 2018, the $1 million Section 162(m) limitation will get harder to avoid. The elimination of the performance-based exception closed a route relied upon historically to circumvent the rules.

As you will find out in the next chapter dedicated to tax-exempt entities, in a similar fashion, the new Act subjects tax-exempt organizations to a 21% percent excise tax (the current corporate rate) on remuneration in excess of $1 million paid to certain 'covered employees.'

QUALIFIED EQUITY GRANTS

 IRC Section 83(i)

The Act includes a new form of income tax

deferral. Beginning in 2018, an employee of a private company who is granted stock options or restricted stock units (RSUs) for services may elect to defer taxes when the equity becomes transferable or vested. The employee can defer income taxation for up to 5 years or until certain events occur, such as an IPO, for instance.

To be eligible for this tax treatment, the corporation must adopt a written plan granting at least 80% of its employees stock options or restricted stock units with the same rights & privileges for all employees. The 80% requirement is met if employees are either granted stock options or RSUs but not a combination of both.

A deferral is not allowed for the CEO, CFO (or anyone who has ever served in those capacities), or family members of those persons, nor for any 1% shareholder or any person who was among the four highest-paid officers in the prior ten years.

Employees must be notified of their deferral right by the employer & a fine of $100 per failure to notify applies.

This new provision leaves in place prior treatment of restricted property, 83(b) elections, incentive stock options & Section 409A considerations for deferred compensation.

A deferral election with respect to an incentive stock option (ISO) eliminates the favorable tax treatment otherwise available for such options.

The deferral period will end if the shares become transferable to the employer or another party, or if they become readily tradable on an established market (i.e., the company goes public), the employee revokes the deferral election, or the employee becomes part of the excluded class. The amount included at the relevant time is determined at the time of exercise of an option or vesting of a grant, as applicable, even if the value is lower at the end of the deferral period. The employer is required to withhold taxes at the highest marginal rate at the end of the deferral period.

If the income tax of the employee is deferred, the corporate compensation deduction is also postponed until the deferred amount is includable in the individual's income, so the employer receives their tax deduction only when the employee recognizes income.

To be eligible for this deferral, a recipient of qualified stock must make an affirmative election (in the same manner as a Section 83(b) election) within 30 days following the date of such stock becoming transferable or no longer subject to a substantial risk of forfeiture, whichever occurs first.

The provision was designed for private companies that give employees equity, which lacks liquidity.

FRINGE BENEFITS

As we already discussed in Chapter 3, the new law:

- Repealed the deductions for entertainment, amusement & recreation, even when directly related to the conduct of business
- Further limited the deductibility of meals
- Disallowed the qualified transportation fringe deduction, unless the expenses are necessary for ensuring the safety of an employee
- Disallowed the deduction for achievement awards
- Suspended the moving expense deduction & the exclusion of relocation reimbursements

Pre-enactment law excluded up to $20 a month in qualified bicycle commuting reimbursement from an employee's gross income. The new law suspends this exclusion for years 2018 through 2025 & requires that any such reimbursements be included in the employee's taxable income, on their w-2.

9 / TAX EXEMPT ORGANIZATIONS

The new tax law includes a few important changes directly affecting tax-exempt organizations.

Most non-profit organizations are tax-exempt under one of the subsections of IRC Section 501(c).

Tax-exempt status means that an organization is exempt from paying federal corporate income tax on income generated from activities that are substantially related to the purposes for which the entity was organized & for which the organization was granted tax-exempt status. The organization must, however, pay federal corporate income tax (at standard corporate tax rates) on income which is unrelated to its tax-exempt purposes, called unrelated business income (UBI). Organizations that meet the requirements for federal tax exemption can generally also rely on that status to exempt their income from state corporate income tax.

Most organizations that are tax-exempt still remain subject to a wide variety of other taxes, including federal payroll taxes, state & local unemployment taxes, real estate taxes, personal property taxes, sales & use taxes, franchise taxes, etc.

UNRELATED BUSINESS INCOME (UBI)

 IRC Section 512(a)(6)

As mentioned earlier, even though an organization is recognized as tax-exempt, it may still be liable for tax on its unrelated business income (UBI). For most organizations, UBI is income from a trade or business, regularly carried on, that is not substantially related to the charitable, educational, or other purpose that is the basis of the organization's exemption.

Under old law, UBI was calculated based on all unrelated business activities, less the deductions directly connected with carrying on these activities, so losses generated by one activity would generally offset income rendered by another activity. Such aggregate or net calculation is no longer allowed.

Under the new law, tax-exempt organizations are required to **separately calculate the net UBI for each unrelated trade or business**. Any loss derived from one unrelated trade or business may not be used to offset income from another.

This change does not apply to any pre tax reform net operating losses (NOLs) generated prior to 2018. These NOLs may be used to reduce aggregate UBI arising from all unrelated activities.

It is somewhat unclear how to determine if a particular activity represents a single or multiple trades or businesses, leaving some space for planning & interpretation.

UBI will be taxed at the rate of 21%.

EXECUTIVE COMPENSATION

 IRC Section 4960

Under the new law, beginning with tax year 2018, tax-exempt organizations are subject to **a brand new 21% excise** tax on:

- Compensation in excess of $1 million per year paid to 'covered employees', which includes the five highest-paid employees,

plus anyone who was a covered employee in 2017
- Separation payments deemed excessive in relation to historic compensation (excess parachute payments) to a covered employee

Employers, not the covered employees, are liable for the excise tax. The tax on compensation over $1 million & the tax on excess parachute payments operate independently. One may apply when the one other does not, but no more than one 21% excise tax may apply to any particular payment.

EXCISE TAX ON ENDOWMENTS

 IRC Section 4968

The bill includes a **new excise tax of 1.4%** on the net investment income of private colleges & universities with:

- at least 500 tuition-paying students during the preceding taxable year, more than 50% of which are located in the United States

- aggregate fair market value (FMV) of the assets at the end of the preceding taxable year of at least $500k per student, not counting assets that are used directly in carrying out the institution's exempt purpose

State colleges & universities are not subject to the tax. Foreign colleges & universities are also exempt unless more than 50% of the tuition-paying students are located in the United States.

If a school is subject to the tax, the law provides that the net investment income will be calculated under rules similar to those applicable to private foundations under IRC Section 4940(c). Private foundations are subject to tax on interest, dividends, realized capital gains, rents, royalties & flow-through income from partnerships. The calculation is adjusted for any income reported as unrelated business taxable income on the IRS form 990-T.

Affected institutions should begin planning how they will determine their investment assets per student & start gathering necessary data.

10 / INDUSTRY IMPACT

The new law may affect some industries more than others as it contains certain tax provisions targeting specific sectors. The major business changes discussed in previous chapters will apply to all US businesses, unless specifically exempt by law. This chapter is focused on tailored, industry-specific parts of the Act & one interesting non-tax provision too.

BANKING / FINANCIAL SERVICES / ASSET MANAGERS

DEDUCTION FOR FDIC PREMIUMS

The new law limits the amount bigger financial institutions may deduct in Federal Deposit Insurance Corporation (FDIC) premiums paid to support the deposit insurance fund, specifically:

- Banks with total consolidated assets between $10 & $50 billion will see a reduction of the deduction
- Banks with total consolidated assets that exceed $50 billion will lose the FDIC deduction completely

CARRIED INTEREST

Carried interest, or 'carry' for short, is a share of the profits received by investment managers, in excess of the percentage that they contributed to the venture - a popular practice in the alternative investments, private equity & hedge fund spaces. It is effectively a fee rewarding the manager for enhancing performance of the investment.

Prior to tax reform, carried interest generated by investments held for more than one year was taxed at a rate of 23.8% (20% long-term capital gain rate + the 3.8% net investment income tax).

Starting with tax year 2018, the **new law requires a three-year holding period** to treat capital gain as long-term for certain partnership interests held in connection with the services performed for a business that consists of:

- Raising or returning capital
- Investing in specified assets or identifying specified assets to invest in
- Developing specified assets

Under the new rule, a taxpayer who holds an applicable partnership interest will be allowed to recognize net long-term capital gain with respect to such interest only if the underlying investment or capital asset was sold by the fund after a holding period of more than three years. If the three-year requirement is not met, the taxpayer's gain will be treated as ordinary income or short-term capital gain, regardless of whether a Section 83(b) election has been made with respect to the carried interest.

Some exceptions exist, however – applicable partnership interests do not include interests held directly by a corporation or interests that provide right to share in capital commensurate with:

- the amount of capital contributed
- or the value of the interest included in income under Section 83 upon receipt or vesting

These exceptions are intended to allow a service partner to earn income as long-term capital gain under the historical rules with respect to a partnership interest received in exchange for contributed capital or to the extent the partner included the value of the interest in income under an 83(b) election. Notwithstanding the foregoing, the House Report explains that a partnership interest will not fail to be treated as transferred or held in connection with the performance of services merely because the taxpayer made contributions to the partnership.

OTHER NOTABLE FINANCIAL ITEMS

- Tax reform repealed the rules related to **tax credit bonds** & the authority to issue new tax credit bonds. The repeal does not affect the tax treatment of existing obligations
- The new law repeals the exclusion from income for interest on **advance refunding bonds** (these are special bonds used to pay principal, interest or the redemption price

on a prior bond issue) for any such bonds issued after 2017

- TCJA **repeals the rollover**, without recognition of income, of capital gains on sale of public company stock when proceeds are used **to acquire stock in specialized small business investment corporations (SSBICs)** within 60 days
- Current law under which interest on **private activity bonds** is excluded from gross income, subject to certain requirements, is retained

INSURANCE

The TCJA includes a bunch of provisions directly & exclusively impacting the insurance industry. When it comes to industry-specific tax reform changes, the insurance sector probably got the most, enough to write a separate book on them.

Insurance tax rules are tricky & complex & it takes a tax pro that specializes in this area to understand them all. Below is a list of the key tax reform items affecting this area, which you can research further if you work in insurance:

- Special NOL rules in Section 172(b)(1)(C)
- Modification to rules for computing life insurance reserves (Section 807)
- Modification to capitalization of deferred acquisition costs (Section 848)
- Modification to life insurance proration rules for purposes of determining dividends received deduction (Section 812)
- Repeal of life insurance company operations losses (Section 810)
- Amendment to definition of life insurance contract (Section 7702)
- New reporting requirement for life settlement transactions & death benefits (Section 6050Y)
- Repeal of small life insurance company deduction (Section 806)
- Repeal of rules for distributions from policyholder surplus accounts (Section 815)
- Modification to discounting rules for unpaid losses (Section 846)
- Modification to proration rules for property & casualty insurance companies (Section 832)

FARMING

Taxpayers engaged in farming may elect out of the new Section 163(j) interest limitation.

An electing farming business is required to use the alternative depreciation system (ADS), with its accompanying restrictions on using bonus depreciation & longer depreciation lives, for any assets with a useful life of more than ten years, including land improvements, barns & other farm buildings.

The Act shortens the cost recovery period from 7 to 5 years for certain machinery / equipment. The law also repeals the required use of the 150% declining balance depreciation method for 3, 5, 7 & 10-year property.

ALCOHOL

The **Craft Beverage Modernization & Tax Reform Act (CBMTRA)** was enacted as part of the tax reform package & provides excise tax relief for calendar years 2018 & 2019 focused on craft producers of alcoholic beverages. The Act introduces special provisions for…

BREWERIES

 IRC Section 5051

Under the bill, the **federal excise tax (FET) is reduced** in half to $3.50/barrel (from $7/barrel) on the first 60,000 barrels for domestic brewers producing less than 2 million barrels annually & reduced to $16/barrel (from $18/barrel) on the first 6 million barrels for all other brewers & all beer importers. The bill would maintain the current $18/barrel rate for barrelage over 6 million.

Additionally, CBMTRA allows the transfer of beer between bonded facilities. Previous law states that beer may be transferred between commonly owned breweries without payment of tax. Under the new bill, all breweries will be able to transfer beers between bonded facilities without tax implications, something that will benefit small unaffiliated brewers & give them the flexibility to collaborate on new beers without facing a tax liability.

Overall, great news for small breweries — for the next couple of years, thanks to these cuts, they should have additional free cash that would otherwise have been paid in excise taxes.

WINERIES

 IRC Section 5041

Wineries can claim an **expanded excise tax credit.** A $1 per gallon federal excise tax credit would be provided for the first 30,000 gallons produced; 90 cents for the next 100,000 gallons & 53.5 cents for the next 620,000 gallons. Producers of sparkling wines now also qualify for the credit.

In the case of wine produced outside of the United States & imported, the Act provides for foreign wine producers to assign the tax credits to importers who elect to receive them.

Wines that are made with a higher percentage of alcohol by volume, 14% to 16%, will now be taxed as other wine at $1.07, down from $1.57 a gallon.

The Act provides that certain 'meads' & 'low alcohol by volume wines' are still deemed wines subject to the wine tax of $1.07 per gallon under Section 5041(b)(1).

Under the old rules, meaderies were subjected to a so-called 'bubble tax,' where higher carbonation resulted in a higher tax.

DISTILLERIES

 IRC Section 5001

The Act provides for **reduced tax rates on distilled spirits**. These rates are equal to $2.70 per proof gallon on the first 100,000 proof gallons & $13.34 per proof gallon on the next 22.13 million proof gallons. The tax rate for distilled spirits not subject to the reduced rates is $13.50 per proof gallon.

In the case of distilled spirits produced abroad & imported, the Act allows foreign manufacturers to assign the reduced tax rates to importers who elect to receive them.

 IRC Section 263A

Additionally, the new law excludes the aging periods for beer, wine & spirits from the production period for purposes of the uniform capitalization (UniCap) interest capitalization rules. As a result, producers can now deduct interest expenses attributable to shorter production periods.

ALASKA DRILLING

The TCJA included a non-tax provision **opening the Arctic National Wildlife Refuge (ANWR) to energy development**. This action, opposed by environmental activists, reverses a 40-year-old policy against developing what could be one of the largest oil fields in US history.

Spanning 19 million acres, about the size of South Carolina, ANWR encompasses Alaska's Northeastern corner. Only about 8% of the refuge has been designated for potential energy development.

Commonly referred to as '1002 area', this relatively small section, could contain over 10 billion barrels of oil, which translates to an oil flow exceeding our country's daily imports from Saudi Arabia.

* * *

ABOUT ME

I'm a licensed New York CPA & an IRS Enrolled Agent. I hold a Masters in Tax from Baruch College in NYC & have been working in tax for 15 years now, combining Big 4 & industry experience.

This book was written in beautiful New York City.

This book may include public domain materials from US government websites like **irs.gov** & information from online publications marked or intended for public release, such as tax alerts.

Use of any copyrighted material constitutes 'fair use' under 17 USC Section 107.

Cover design, interior design & typesetting **by Timur Knyazev, CPA**.

Icons used throughout this book are free for personal & commercial use & are distributed **by Icons8.com**.

Cover art (the hipster) **by Luis Shmoo**.

Made in the USA
Middletown, DE
16 February 2019